The Mystery
of the Phantom Ship

Laura E. Williams

SCHOLASTIC INC.

New York Toronto London Auckland Sydney
Mexico City New Delhi Hong Kong Buenos Aires

For Jennifer Jones and Richard Welling

A Roundtable Press Book

For Roundtable Press, Inc.:
Directors: Julie Merberg, Marsha Melnick, Susan E. Meyer
Project Editor: Meredith Wolf Schizer
Editorial Assistant: Sara Newberry
Designer: Elissa Stein
Illustrator: Laura Hartman Maestro

ISBN 0-439-21729-6

12 11 10 9 8 7 6 5 4 3 2   2 3 4 5 6/0

Printed in the U.S.A.
First Scholastic printing, September 2001

Contents

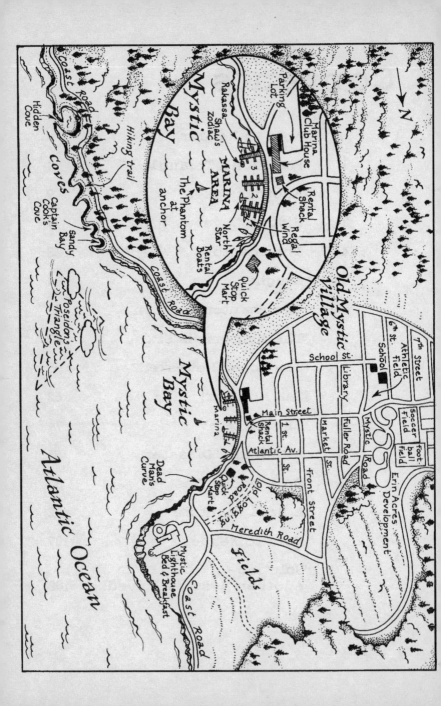

Note to Reader

Welcome to *The Mystery of the Phantom Ship*, where YOU solve the mystery. As you read, look for clues pointing to the guilty person. There is a blank suspect sheet in the back of this book. You can copy it to keep track of the clues you find throughout the story. It is the same as the suspect sheets that Jen and Zeke will use later in the story when they try to solve the mystery. Can you solve *The Mystery of the Phantom Ship* before they do?

Good luck!

Poseidon's Triangle

"They've been out there for a long time," Stacey said, checking the glow-in-the-dark dial on her watch.

Jen scanned the moonlit horizon for any sign of the sailing sloop her twin brother, Zeke, was crewing. "The *North Star* should be back soon."

Tommy and Stacey, the twins' best friends, sat restlessly on either side of Jen on the gray, weather-beaten Mystic Marina bench. Because of Saturday's big sailing race, there were a lot of visitors in the small Maine town. The usually quiet marina bustled with tourists admiring the boats and exploring the waterfront area.

Tommy snorted. "The crew needs all the practice it can get without me on the team."

Jen jabbed him in the ribs. "Don't be a sore loser."

"I didn't lose," Tommy sputtered. "I'm telling you, someone tricked me off the team. I'm one of the best sailors around."

"True," Jen agreed. Zeke and Tommy had both wanted to earn the only junior spot on the crew of the *North Star,* but Tommy had missed one of the practices, so the captain had disqualified him. There were still three other kids fighting it out against Zeke for the junior position. Mystic's team was the only one in the race that let a kid be a member of the crew.

"It would be so cool if Zeke got on the crew," Jen said, thinking out loud.

"Without me to challenge him," Tommy said, "he probably will."

"Imagine getting five hundred thousand dollars just for winning a sailboat race!" Stacey said. "Even if the crew doesn't get to keep it, that's still half a million!" The hometown marina and the owner of the winning boat split the earnings, usually rewarding the boat's crew with a big feast after the race.

"Every team wants to win," Jen said. "Who wouldn't?" Sailboats were already arriving at the Mystic Marina for the annual event. By tomorrow, there would be dozens of boats up and down the entire east coast. Already boats from as far away as South Carolina and Florida were moored at the docks. Last year, the race had been held in Newport, Rhode Island. But since Mystic won that race—for the first time in twenty-five years—they got to host the race this year.

Tommy sighed. "If I were on the *North Star* crew, I'd do anything to win."

Stacey widened her light blue eyes and peered around Jen. "Anything?"

"Anything," Tommy said firmly. "Even though I wouldn't get the money, it'd be such an honor. I could crew on any boat I wanted to after that. Captains would beg me to work for them."

Jen chuckled. "I thought the all-star baseball teams were going to be begging for you."

With a wide smile, Tommy said, "No problem. I'll do both!"

The three of them laughed. Even though Tommy was bragging, Jen had to admit he was an excellent sailor and baseball player. But everyone also knew that he was best at eating. As if to prove it, he stood up and headed for the clubhouse.

"Anyone want a hot dog?" Tommy called over his shoulder.

Jen and Stacey shook their heads, then Jen caught sight of Captain Till, the director of Mystic Marina. She pointed him out to her friend.

"What's he doing?" Stacey asked.

Jen shrugged. The brawny man with white hair and full white beard and mustache was pacing up and down a nearby dock. Suddenly he turned with a frown on his face, quickly scanned the area, then walked away, disappearing into the nighttime shadows.

"He looks upset," Jen said.

"He's probably wondering what happened to the *North Star*," Stacey said, turning to look at Jen. "And so am I."

"Stop worrying," Jen said, patting her friend on the knee. "You're making me nervous, too." Just the thought of sailing on a dark ocean gave her the creeps. Even sailing in broad daylight didn't thrill her. Not that she was afraid of water, but something about the rocking motion of sailboats always made her nauseous.

"What are you kids up to?" a gruff voice asked.

Jen flinched. It took her a second to realize it was Captain Till, the man they'd just seen pacing the dock.

"We're waiting for the *North Star*," she explained, wondering why he was creeping around and sneaking up on them.

Captain Till's brows pulled together as he glanced at his watch. "They should be back by now. I hope nothing's happened out there."

Jen swallowed the lump of fear she'd been trying to ignore. "I'm sure they're fine," she said, trying to sound confident.

"I don't know," Captain Till said doubtfully. "I've spent many years out on the sea, and terrible things can occur." He put one foot up on the bench and leaned forward, raking his fingers through his beard. "I remember once when a gale blew up out of nowhere. Nearly flipped us over, it did. As it was, one of the fellows got swept right over the edge into a watery grave."

Jen shivered. Captain Till was known for his frightening tales of the sea, but did he have to tell one right now?

"And then there's Poseidon's Triangle," the captain continued. "That's a dangerous piece of ocean. Why, I've heard of giant sea monsters swallowing cargo ships in one gulp. One time I saw it happen with my own eyes. A barge carrying fifty tons of iron ore disappeared . . . just like *that*." He snapped his fingers. "I even saw an enormous tentacle rise out of the water where the barge had been not two seconds before. We never saw the barge or the men on board again, and—"

"I'm sure the *North Star* is fine," Jen interrupted, willing it to be true. She didn't want to hear any more stories of monsters in Poseidon's Triangle. The "piece of ocean" Captain Till was talking about was a triangular area of unusually rough water just off the coast of Mystic. Everyone in Mystic had heard legends of ships disappearing, and sea monsters lurking, and other sea disasters happening there. It wasn't marked, but sailors knew approximately where it was, and they were all very careful to avoid it.

"Don't worry, missy," Captain Till said with a chuckle. "I made sure the race route stays far away from the Triangle."

Jen didn't feel relieved. She knew how bossy the wind could be. It could push a boat where it had no intention of going, if the crew wasn't alert at all times.

Captain Till rubbed his hands together. "Aye, I can feel it in me bones," he said, sounding like a pirate.

"Feel what?" Tommy asked, returning with his mouth stuffed full of hot dog.

"The *North Star* is going to win the race this year," Captain Till said firmly.

Jen hoped so too, but how could he be so sure? "How do you know?"

The older gentleman looked at her and winked. "I told you, I feel it in me bones." With a nod, he trotted back toward the marina.

"That guy looks like Santa Claus," Tommy said,

wiping a smear of ketchup off his chin.

"He's kind of creepy to be Santa," Stacey said, twisting a blond curl around her finger. "Santa doesn't go around scaring kids with stories of sea monsters!"

Jen silently agreed with her best friend. *And where was the* North Star *anyway? Why hadn't it sailed into the harbor yet? Had a sea serpent swallowed it whole?* Even though she knew she was being ridiculous, she couldn't shake the feeling of doom.

She tried to tune into her twin sensor. Sometimes she knew what Zeke was going to say before he opened his mouth. Or sometimes she could sense what he was feeling even when he was miles away.

Dread lodged itself in her stomach. Something was wrong with Zeke. She just *knew* it.

Zeke looked out over the Atlantic. With the moon near full, and only a few clouds in the sky, the ocean twinkled like a bucket full of diamonds. The wind filled the sails, and the water slapped against the hull of the *North Star*. So far, the "test sail" had gone smoothly. Zeke and three other kids—Liz, Chris, and Clara—were being watched and tested on this trip by Captain Billy Saber and Mrs. Horn. Zeke felt he'd done very well. He worked quickly, listened to orders, and kept the ropes and gear neatly stowed when not in use. He thought he had a good chance of being chosen as the only junior crew member.

Then why did he feel a prickle of unease crawl up his back? He tried to shake away the feeling.

Maybe it had something to do with Poseidon's Triangle just to their west. Not that he was superstitious or anything, but after growing up hearing all the awful tales of giant sea creatures, strange crosscurrents, dangerous whirlpools, and even phantom pirate ships, it was no wonder the Triangle made him a little jumpy.

Instead of squeezing between the Triangle and Maine's rocky coast, they were sailing toward Mystic, on the far side of the Triangle. As soon as they passed the treacherous piece of ocean, they would cut west and head into the harbor. No problem.

"No problem," he repeated out loud, but the wind whipped the words out of his mouth, and even he didn't hear them. Sitting on the deck, he forced himself to relax his spine and loosen his clenched fists.

In an instant, his whole body tensed up again. Off the port side of the *North Star* he saw lights. Was he imagining it? No, he clearly saw the outline of a sleek sailboat as it slid silently through the water—*right in the middle of Poseidon's Triangle*. Only a second later, the boat had disappeared!

Another Joke?

"Captain!" Zeke called, scrambling to his feet. "Captain, come here!"

"What is it?" the tall, lanky captain asked as he made his way to Zeke's side. "See a sea monster in the Triangle?" He laughed.

"No . . . but I did see a sailboat."

Captain Saber frowned, squinting his eyes. "Where?"

Zeke pointed. "Right out there, sir. It appeared suddenly, and a second later it was gone. Looked like it was sucked into the ocean."

"Are you pulling my leg?" the captain asked, giving Zeke a hard look.

"No, I swear. I saw it."

Captain Saber shouted to the other crew members. "Come about!"

Immediately, the crew scampered into action.

"Where are we going?" Liz asked. "I thought we were headed home."

"Zeke saw a boat in Poseidon's Triangle. We have to check it out, to make sure nothing's happened."

"We're going in there?" Chris asked, alarm in his voice. The short, redheaded boy was in a few of Zeke's sixth-grade classes at Mystic Middle School, but it seemed like Zeke was seeing him everywhere ever since the competition had started a few weeks ago.

"No choice," the captain said gruffly.

"When we don't find anything, you'll get kicked off the team," Liz said under her breath, smirking at Zeke. Tall, with a neat, blond ponytail, Liz acted like she was much more than just two years older than Zeke. She also acted like she'd already been chosen for the junior position.

Even Clara, the seventh grader who kept to herself and peered quietly at everyone through wire-rimmed glasses, gave him a dirty look. "Good going, Zeke," she muttered.

Zeke tried to ignore the comments. The rigging creaked as the boat turned into the Triangle. He kept his eyes wide, searching the water for any sign of a shipwreck—waving hands, a loose flotation vest, a scrap of wood, anything. . . .

After a few minutes, Captain Saber said, "I don't see anything. You sure about the boat, Zeke?"

Zeke swallowed. He *thought* he was sure. But that didn't explain how the boat had disappeared into thin air like a phantom. He tried to picture the boat, but a vision of leaping dolphins came to mind instead of the sleek sailboat he thought he'd seen. "Well," he admitted reluctantly, "I thought I was. But maybe it was only a pod of dolphins."

"Dolphins? Why didn't you say so in the first place? Let's get out of the Triangle," Captain Saber said angrily. He gave the order to come about again.

The crew quickly steered the boat back toward the Mystic harbor. Soon after, they lowered the sails and motored into their berth beside dock two. Zeke waved to Jen, Stacey, and Tommy, who were waiting for him, but he couldn't leave until everything was stowed, the sails rolled and tied, and the decks hosed off.

"Finally," Jen exclaimed, when he hopped over the side and onto the dock.

"Worried?" Liz taunted before Zeke could say anything.

Jen narrowed her eyes at the older girl competing for the same job as her brother. "No," she lied. "It's just getting late and we have school tomorrow."

Liz sighed loudly. "You can blame it on Zeke."

Then she looked at Tommy and smiled. "Too bad you missed practice and got kicked off the team. I could have used some competition." With that, she flipped her long ponytail and sauntered up the dock.

Tommy glared after her.

Clara slid past the four of them without a word, but Chris stopped. "Girls are so stupid," the redhead said, motioning toward Liz.

"Yup," Tommy agreed. "She's probably the one who called to tell me that practice was canceled when it really wasn't. Liz just wanted me to get kicked off the team, and she knew the only way to do it was by tricking me." He lowered his voice. "But Captain Saber didn't believe that I got that phone call."

"That's because you couldn't prove it," Stacey reminded him.

Tommy spread his hands. "I swear it. Someone called, saying she was Ms. Myers or Matthews or something from the marina and that Captain Saber had told her to call us all to cancel practice. Why would I make that up?"

"Maybe he thought you were just being your lazy old self," Stacey teased.

"Very funny," Tommy grumbled.

Chris said, "Liz thinks she's going to win the junior position." He turned to Zeke. "But I know *you're* going to win it because you're the best."

"Uh, thanks," Zeke said, his mind not totally on the conversation. He was used to Liz's stuck-up attitude, and he had more important things to worry about.

"Well, gotta go study for the test tomorrow. See you then," Chris said, and he hurried away.

"What did Liz mean when she blamed you for the *North Star* docking late?" Jen asked, eyeing her brother.

Zeke took a deep breath, not sure his sister and friends would believe what he saw. He wasn't so sure he believed it himself. "I saw a phantom ship!"

Jen gasped. "What?"

They started walking toward the marina so Zeke could get his backpack out of his locker. "I saw a sail-boat right in the middle of Poseidon's Triangle. One minute it was there, the next it was gone."

"You must have imagined it," Stacey said.

"Are you sure you saw it?" Jen asked.

Zeke shrugged. "I'm pretty sure I saw it. But when we went into the Triangle to look, we didn't see anything."

"Maybe someone was playing a joke on you," Tommy said.

"Like the ropes you found on the *North Star* that were tied in knots and soaked in seawater?" Jen asked.

Zeke groaned. How could he forget the hours it

had taken him to untie them? And the worst part was that Captain Saber had said Zeke was responsible for the problem by not securing them properly, even though he was sure he had.

"Maybe it was a joke," he agreed thoughtfully.

They walked through the front lobby of the marina clubhouse toward the locker rooms. Tommy stopped in front of the glass cabinet and admired the gold trophy Mystic had won in last year's race.

"Maybe we'll win it again," Stacey said, looking at

the gold cup with the sailboat engraved on its side.

"I hope so," Jen added. She wondered briefly why Captain Till had sounded so sure of himself earlier.

Zeke hurried to the men's locker room to retrieve his backpack. When he reached his locker, he frowned. The dark green metal door to Number 34 was partially open. "I thought I locked it," he said to the empty room. He shrugged. Grabbing his bag, he flung it over one shoulder and carefully closed the locker door. Then he twirled the dial, double-checking that it was locked securely.

In the lobby, only Jen was still waiting for him. "Stacey and Tommy had to go home," she explained. "We'd better get going, too. Aunt Bee will be worried, even though I called her about an hour ago."

Aunt Bee owned the Mystic Lighthouse Bed and Breakfast just outside town. Jen and Zeke had lived there with her since their parents died in a car accident nine years before, when the twins were just two. The twins never wanted to worry Aunt Bee, since she had enough to do taking care of the lighthouse guests.

When Jen and Zeke stepped outside, it took a moment for their eyes to adjust to the dim light from the single lamps at the end of each dock. Aside from a few voices wafting over from some of the boats, all was quiet. By now, most of the tourists had gone to bed at the various inns and motels around town. All the rooms at the B&B were full with visitors in town for the race.

Jen suddenly grabbed Zeke's arm. "What's that?" She pointed to pier two.

Zeke peered into the shadows. A crouched figure in dark clothing was silently stepping onto the deck of the *North Star*.

Hidden Cove

"Come on," Zeke whispered. "Let's see what he's up to." He took off toward the pier, his pack bouncing against his back.

Jen followed her twin closely. When they reached the wooden dock they slowed down to keep their sneakers from thudding on the boards and alerting the trespasser.

As they crept forward, Jen could barely make out a shadow moving around on the boat. Just as they reached the lines holding the *North Star* to the dock, the crouched figure spotted them and jumped off the boat. He shoved the twins apart and ran between them and up the dock. Jen fell sideways, catching herself on the low railing. Zeke stumbled, but regained his footing.

The intruder's dark form disappeared into the

black shadows beyond the marina.

"Are you okay?" Zeke asked, helping Jen to her feet.

"I'm fine. But when I get my hands on that jerk, he'll see what it feels like to be knocked down!"

Zeke laughed.

Jen glared at him. "What's so funny?"

"You, when you're mad. You pretend to be fierce, but when it comes down to it, you're more of a pussy-cat than Slinky," he said, referring to their pet Maine coon cat.

"What's going on?" asked an angry voice. They whirled around to see Captain Saber striding down the dock toward them. "What are you two doing out here? You know you're not supposed to be anywhere near the boat when no one's on board."

"We saw a trespasser on the *North Star*," Zeke explained. "We followed him out here."

Captain Saber frowned. "Who was it?"

"We couldn't tell," Jen said. "As soon as we got close to the boat, he jumped off and knocked us down. I almost fell into the water."

"Well, it's too dangerous out here at night for a couple of kids. I'm sure your aunt wouldn't want you out here at this hour. Now go on home. I'd hate to count this against you, Zeke."

Jen opened her mouth to protest, but Zeke tugged

her away. He knew better than to argue with Captain Saber. He was sure the captain thought he was the one pulling the pranks, like tying the ropes. He probably even thought Zeke had made up seeing the sailboat in Poseidon's Triangle. Zeke sighed. At this rate, he'd never get chosen to be a crew member on the *North Star*.

Silently, the twins retrieved their bikes. As soon as they got out of town they could see the lighthouse beacon burning bright on the distant bluff. Jen loved the way it seemed to welcome her home. Even though the lighthouse wasn't officially in use anymore, Aunt Bee liked to keep the light flashing. She said it added to the old-time feel of the B&B.

After they finally made it up the steep driveway to the B&B, they parked their bikes and hurried inside.

"I'm in here," Aunt Bee called from the large dining room. When they appeared, she smiled at them. "I'm just getting ready for the prerace banquet on Friday night. With so many guests to take care of, I just know I won't have time to decorate if I wait until the last minute." She continued hanging a string of small, anchor-shaped lights.

"Do you want some help?" Zeke asked.

"Heavens no," Aunt Bee said. "You must have

some homework to do, and it's already so late. Relax, then go to bed. Only three days till the big race!"

The twins hugged their aunt good night and made their way to the circular museum that filled the first floor of the lighthouse tower. Jen's bedroom was on the second floor of the tower, and Zeke's occupied the third. Before he died, the twins' uncle Cliff had renovated the tower for them.

As they climbed the stairs, Jen paused and took a deep breath. "I think we have to explore Poseidon's Triangle tomorrow."

"Are you crazy?"

"We have to look for a clue to what you saw tonight. I don't think it was just your imagination, and neither do you. You don't want anything strange to happen and ruin the race, do you? We've got to find out what happened to that ship."

"But what about your seasickness?"

Jen's stomach turned just thinking about it. "This is more important."

"Okay," Zeke agreed. "We can take out a Zodiac tomorrow. Motorboats don't make you as sick as sailboats. We can check out the Triangle, but no way are we going *into* it. Captain Saber made us sail around in it tonight, and it was really scary."

Jen agreed, secretly relieved. Though she knew it

was a myth, she didn't want to risk being swallowed by a sea monster with giant tentacles, or being sucked into a mysterious whirlpool, never to be heard from again.

Zeke left Jen at her door and climbed the next flight of stairs up to his room. The stairs circled one flight farther up to the open platform on top of the lighthouse tower.

In his room, which was decorated with race car posters and *Star Wars* memorabilia neatly arranged on his bookshelves, Zeke stretched and yawned. He didn't have any schoolwork, but he did need to study for the written test Captain Saber was giving tomorrow. The captain was making it as tough as possible to win the junior position.

Zeke sat on his bed and opened his book bag. He riffled through the neatly filed books and papers, looking for the notes he'd taken during the weeks of practice. Feeling a bit uneasy, he looked through everything a second time; all his books were exactly where he'd put them, but his crew notes were gone. With panic tightening his throat, he dumped the bag onto his bedspread. Several pens and pencils, four books, papers, a few pebbles, and some empty candy wrappers lay scattered before him. But no notes!

Heart hammering, he shuffled through every

book and every scrap of paper. His notes were definitely missing. Groaning, Zeke realized that now he'd have to go through the crew book and take new notes to study from before tomorrow. He glanced at the clock beside his bed. 10:00 P.M. He had a late night ahead if he wanted to make the team.

~~

Thursday after school, Zeke dragged himself down to the marina where he was supposed to meet Jen.

"What's wrong with you?" she asked, looking at him.

He yawned. "I couldn't find my notes in my backpack last night, so I had to go through the entire book again." He yawned a second time.

Jen yawned, too. "Hey, cut that out. Yawns are contagious, you know, and I'm not even tired. What happened to your notes? Did you leave them somewhere?"

Zeke shook his head. "That's the weird thing. I'm sure they were in my backpack after school." He shrugged. "No use worrying about it now. I'm ready for the test." He headed into the marina clubhouse. "But if we're going to check out Poseidon's Triangle, we'd better go now. I don't want to be late. Captain Saber said the test starts in the marina conference room at five o'clock sharp."

Jen checked her watch. "That gives us at least an hour and a half. Let's go."

They signed out an inflatable Zodiac and put on their life vests. Then Zeke pulled the cord to start the motor's engine. Just as it sputtered to life, Captain Till waved at them from the far end of the dock.

"Hang on, kids," he called.

Zeke put the engine into idle while they waited for the white-haired man to jog over to them.

"Where are you off to?" Captain Till asked.

"Just going out for a little cruise," Zeke said. "The water is so smooth, it's the perfect day for it."

"Just stay away from those southern coves," the captain warned, scratching his beard. "Very dangerous currents down around there."

Jen nodded, wondering why he was telling them this. Everyone in Mystic knew about the currents around the southern coves, but that didn't stop people from exploring them in nice weather and at low tide.

"And, of course, stay away from Poseidon's Triangle." He winked.

"Aye aye, sir," Zeke said, saluting. With that, he eased the Zodiac away from the dock.

When Jen looked back, Captain Till was still standing there, watching them.

"What was that all about?" she wondered out loud.

"He likes to think he's everyone's grandfather. You know, watching out for us," Zeke said, the wind whipping through his wavy, brown hair as he opened up the throttle.

Jen held on for dear life as the motorized dinghy slapped the waves and spray speckled her face. She squinted to keep the salt out of her eyes. Knowing it wouldn't do any good to try to talk over the engine, she made a mental note to tell Zeke what Captain Till had said last night. The head of the marina had seemed so sure the *North Star* would win the race again this year. Why?

The Zodiac sprang into the air and smashed down so hard, it rattled all thoughts out of Jen's head. Zeke hooted with joy. Jen swallowed hard. *I will not throw up, I will not throw up*, she repeated silently.

At last, Zeke eased the pressure on the throttle, and the small rubber motorboat slowed down as they turned south out of the Mystic harbor. The coves cut into the coast on the right, and Poseidon's Triangle sat to the left like an invisible sea monster, waiting to pounce if they got too close.

"I don't think we'll find anything in the Triangle," Zeke shouted above the motor. "But keep your eyes open just in case."

"Let's check out the coves, too," Jen suggested. "If there was an accident, maybe something washed up in one of them."

Zeke nodded. There were dozens of coves along this stretch of coast. He still enjoyed exploring them, and so did Jen when he could get her into a boat. When they were younger, they used to play pirates there for hours at a time.

The first inlet was called Sandy Bay. Why, Zeke had no idea. There wasn't a speck of sand in sight, just jagged cliffs dropping straight down into the choppy Atlantic. Zeke decided that the next cove, Captain Cook's Cove, was named by someone who liked alliteration. When they popped back out of Captain Cook's Cove, Zeke turned the Zodiac south again.

By the sixth small cove, Jen had had about enough. "Maybe we should head back," she said before Zeke opened up the throttle again, making it impossible to be heard over the motor.

"Let's just hit one more," Zeke said. "My favorite is next. Hidden Cove."

Jen shrugged. Her stomach actually felt fine. "Okay," she agreed. Hidden Cove cut into the coast just three minutes south. It was called Hidden Cove because from the ocean it looked like a shallow depression in the face of the cliff. But really, just on the other side of a large, jutting rock, there lay a big deepwater cove with rocky beaches.

As they veered around the rock, they saw that the cove was as empty as all the others had been. No pieces of wrecked sailboat bobbed in the waves; no oil slicked the surface of the water from a sunken, leaking gas tank; no stranded survivors waved to them from the shore. Their mission had been little more than a waste of time.

"Wait a minute," Jen shouted, just as Zeke was

about to head out again. She pointed toward the rocky beach.

He aimed the boat in that direction. Not until they were much closer did he see what his sister had spotted from much farther away: the remains of a bonfire.

"It's still smoking a little," Jen said.

Zeke nodded. "Weird place for a campfire."

"Maybe a family camped out here last night. Or it could have been some teenagers from the high school."

Zeke bumped the dinghy against the shore, and Jen jumped out with a pail. She filled it with salt water and quickly doused the fire until it stopped smoking.

They didn't find anything else in the cove, so they headed back to the marina. Jen kept her eyes directed toward the sea, searching for anything out of the ordinary in or near Poseidon's Triangle.

As they pulled into the calmer water of the harbor, Zeke suddenly slowed down. Jen turned and gave him a questioning look.

"That sailboat," Zeke said, pointing to the harbor. "That's the one I saw last night in Poseidon's Triangle!"

The Phantom

Shocked, Jen stared at the sleek vessel that was anchored in the middle of the harbor. No one was on deck. "Are you sure?" she asked.

"Definitely," Zeke said. "When I saw the sailboat, I could have sworn I saw dolphins jumping out of the water. Look at the figurehead. That's what was so strange about it last night," he said, recalling what he'd seen.

Jen admired the beautifully carved dolphins that seemed to leap from the bow of the boat. The white boat looked awesome with the graceful, blue-painted dolphins emerging from the prow.

"When was the last time you saw a boat with a figurehead?" Zeke asked.

"Never," Jen admitted.

"Exactly," Zeke said. "And that explains why I

thought it might have been a pod of dolphins I saw instead of a boat."

Jen slowly shook her head. "It doesn't make sense."

"Why not?"

"This boat wasn't here last night. If you really saw this boat in Poseidon's Triangle last night, it would have arrived before, or just after, the *North Star* pulled into the harbor. How do you explain that?"

Zeke frowned. "But I know I saw those dolphins."

"Maybe what you saw really *was* a pod of dolphins," Jen reasoned. "Your eyesight isn't that great."

Zeke didn't answer. He steered the Zodiac closer to the moored ship. The carved dolphins looked real. Maybe Jen was right. He just *thought* they were the same dolphins he'd seen last night. *But I know I saw the outline of a ship*, he thought. He caught sight of the boat's name carefully painted on the stern. His breath caught in his throat.

Jen gasped. She saw the name, too.

The Phantom.

The twins looked at each other with wide blue eyes.

"How strange is that?" Jen said, her voice barely above a whisper.

Zeke turned the outboard motor so that the inflatable dinghy veered away from *The Phantom*, heading toward the docks. He suddenly didn't want anything to do with that boat. It creeped him out. He'd seen a pod of dolphins last night; that would have to be a good enough explanation for him. Besides, he had to concentrate on his test. It was about to begin.

After they tied up the Zodiac and signed it back in at the boathouse, the twins headed for the main clubhouse building. Before they reached it, Tommy came running toward them.

Breathless, he gasped, "The trophy was stolen!"

"What trophy?" Zeke asked, still walking. He didn't want to be late for the test.

"The racing trophy Mystic won last year!"

Zeke stopped in his tracks. "From the glass case?"

Tommy nodded, catching his breath.

"Who'd want to steal that?" Jen asked. "It's not like you could put it on your mantel or anything."

The three of them hurried into the clubhouse. A small crowd had gathered around the empty case. Captain Till stood in the middle of the commotion, nervously tugging at his white beard.

Zeke shook his head. "I can't believe someone would steal it." He checked his watch. He didn't have time to stand around; if he was late, Captain Saber would kick him out of the competition. "I'll see you after the test," he said to Jen.

"Good luck," she said, squeezing his arm. He disappeared into the growing crowd, and Jen turned back to the empty case. She caught a glimpse of Stacey in the middle of the crowd with her reporter's notebook in hand, questioning people about whether they'd seen anything suspicious.

"They should've locked the cabinet," Tommy said.

Jen didn't agree. Mystic was such a safe town, even unlocked bikes didn't get stolen. Who would ever think the famous trophy would disappear?

Captain Till's booming voice rose above the hubbub of the crowd. "This is disgraceful," he bellowed. "We will be the laughingstock of the racing world. The cup was stolen right out from under our noses!"

Jen tried to shrug off an uneasy feeling. Too many strange things were happening. All the "jokes" on the *North Star*, the mysterious dolphins Zeke saw last night, the hunched figure lurking on the docks, and now this.

Stacey interrupted her thoughts with a jab in the stomach with her pencil. "Did you see anything suspicious?"

"When?" Jen asked, wondering if the campfire in Hidden Cove or *The Phantom* would be considered suspicious by anyone except her. "Where?"

Stacey rolled her eyes. "Here, silly. Did you see anything that might lead to the capture of the thief?"

"No," Jen said. "It was still in the case last night, remember? Someone must have stolen it today."

"I've already figured that out," Stacey said, checking her notes. "I'm going to go write this up for the school paper. See you later." Without even a wave, she took off.

As Jen watched her go, something else caught her eye. An unfamiliar person was standing off to the side, near the glass doors at the exit. He had salt-and-pepper-colored hair that fell over his forehead, and he was short. No, Jen realized as she stepped to the side when someone blocked her view, he wasn't short, but hunched over.

With a stab of alarm, she realized that this was the man who had been on the docks and climbed aboard the *North Star* last night. He hadn't been crouching; it looked like his spine was permanently curved forward. The more she stared at him, the more familiar he looked. Hadn't she seen him somewhere else *before* last night?

She nudged Tommy in the ribs. "Don't look now," she said out of the side of her mouth. "But there's a guy standing over there."

Tommy whirled around. "The hunched guy? What about him?"

"I said *not* to look!" Jen hissed.

All of a sudden, the man spotted them staring at him. He quickly turned around and left through the double doors.

"Have you ever seen that man before?" Jen asked Tommy, craning her neck, trying to keep an eye on him.

"Sure," Tommy said. "He's been around here for days. I figured he was with one of the crews that sailed in early."

Then why was he snooping around the North Star? Jen wondered. "I'm going to follow him," she said as the man disappeared from view.

"Whatever floats your boat," Tommy said with a one-shouldered shrug. "Me, I'm going to get something to eat." He headed for the cafeteria.

But before Jen could take a single step after the hunched man, someone grabbed her arm. She jerked around. Zeke stood beside her, his face pale, reddish brown freckles popping out on his nose and cheeks.

"What's wrong?" Jen exclaimed.

Her brother didn't say anything. He just held up the blue gym bag he kept in his locker at the marina. It was zipped closed.

She didn't understand. "What?"

"Look inside," he whispered nervously.

Baffled, Jen took the bag. It felt heavy. Slowly she unzipped a corner. "Oh, no!"

5

Caught!

Zeke watched his sister's eyes widen in horror as she stared at the missing cup in his bag.

"Where did you find this?" she asked in a hushed voice. She quickly rezipped the bag.

"It was in my locker. My *locked* locker. Someone put it in my gym bag."

Jen handed him the bag. "That *someone* is trying to get you kicked out of the competition."

"That's what I figure, too." He shook his head, thinking. "But I don't know who it could be."

"It must be Liz," Jen said immediately, keeping her voice low. "She thinks she's so great. She's always bragging that she's going to win the junior competition."

"Maybe," Zeke agreed. "But Clara is so quiet, who knows what she's thinking?"

"And Chris isn't the type. In fact, he keeps saying

he thinks you're going to win."

Zeke sighed. "I may never find out. Anyway, how can I turn this in?" he asked, motioning to the bag. "Who's going to believe it got wrapped in a towel with my name on it and hidden in my locker? Captain Saber will kick me out of the competition for sure."

Jen bit her lower lip and looked around to make sure no one was paying attention to them. "Give it to me," she said. "I'll take care of it. You have to take the test."

Reluctantly, he handed her the bag. "What are you going to do about it? It's my problem, not yours."

"Don't worry. I'll figure something out. You have to take the test and pass it. That's the most important thing right now. Hurry, or you'll be late."

Zeke hesitated. "Thanks, sis."

Jen laughed. "Don't worry, you'll owe me big time for this."

Zeke hurried toward the conference room at the back of the clubhouse. He was the last one to enter and sit down.

Captain Saber glared at him and checked his watch. "One second to spare, Zeke. Glad you could join us."

Glowing red, Zeke pulled a pencil out of his back pocket and waited silently for the test to be placed in front of him.

"You have two hours," the captain stated before

sitting in a chair in the front of the room where he could keep an eye on the four participants.

Zeke bent his head over the test and wrote his name in the upper right corner. That was the easy part.

1. What is the jib sheet and when is it used?

It wasn't that the questions were so difficult, Zeke realized as he scanned the test. It was that he kept expecting to hear shouts of "Thief! Thief!" echoing down the hall and into the conference room. He couldn't help imagining Jen getting arrested for stealing the gold cup. How would she return it without getting caught? What would Aunt Bee say when she had to go to the police station to pick her up? They'd both be grounded for life. Then he reconsidered. Aunt Bee was fair. She wouldn't punish them until she'd heard the whole story. But who would believe that someone else put the gold cup in his locker, which he'd carefully locked last night?

He stared down at the test paper. So far he hadn't answered a single question.

Who put the trophy in my locker?

He peeked sideways at Clara, not wanting Captain Saber to think he was cheating. Totally involved in the test, she didn't even notice him looking. He shook his head. She didn't seem like the type to do something so rotten.

He glanced in the other direction, toward Liz. She, on the other hand, seemed like the perfect candidate. Liz was one of the most competitive people he'd ever met.

Finally he looked over at Chris, who was chewing on the end of his pencil and staring at the ceiling.

Zeke returned his attention to his test paper, but he couldn't stop thinking about the gold cup. He knew *why* someone had done this to him. If only he could figure out *who*!

Tapping his eraser on the desk, he imagined the thief stealing the cup, creeping into the locker room . . .

Zeke jerked straight up in his chair. *Of course!* At last he knew who had been playing all the "jokes" and who had planted the trophy in his gym bag to get him kicked out of the competition. There was nothing he could do about it now, but just knowing who the culprit was made him feel better.

He still didn't hear any commotion outside by the trophy case, and he finally began to relax. His mind focused. He started writing, and he didn't stop until Captain Saber said, "Time's up," two hours later.

Jen clutched Zeke's bulky gym bag in her right hand as she walked through the clubhouse. Would someone figure out what was in it? After all, a giant cup looked like a giant cup, even hidden in a bag. Keeping her eyes peeled, she searched for Tommy. She'd need his help to get the trophy back where it belonged without getting caught and being blamed for the theft.

"Figures I'd find you here," she said when she finally located him next to the ice-cream machine in the cafeteria. He'd just made himself a double swirl cone and topped it with chocolate sprinkles.

"Want a bite?" Tommy offered.

Jen shook her head. "I need your help."

"Sure. Just let me finish this." He took a giant lick off the top of the cone.

"I need your help *now*," Jen said, leaning toward him. She whispered to Tommy what had happened.

"Why did he steal it?" Tommy asked when she'd finished.

"Who?"

"Zeke."

Jen clenched her teeth. "*Zeke* didn't take the trophy."

"But you said it's in his gym bag," Tommy said, pointing with his ice cream toward the bag Jen still clutched in her hand.

"Someone *else* put it in there. Like how someone called to tell you that practice was canceled?"

"Oh," Tommy said, obviously understanding at last. Then he scowled. "I'll bet it was Liz."

"We don't have time to figure that out now," Jen said. "I want to get rid of this thing, the sooner the better. Listen, here's my idea."

When she finished explaining her plan, Tommy grinned. "I think I can do that."

"I'm depending on you," Jen said earnestly. "Count to fifteen, then start." When Tommy nodded, Jen hurried back to the front lobby, counting slowly to fifteen along the way.

Just as she neared the empty glass cabinet, she heard a loud shout come down the hall.

"Ugh! A rat!" Tommy shouted. "I saw a really big, ugly rat!"

The people still lingering around the cabinet rushed away, heading for the cafeteria.

Tommy kept yelling, and pretty soon other loud voices joined in.

"Where'd it go?"

"Help! I hate rats!"

"I just saw it go that way!"

"Eeek!"

"Gross!"

Jen smiled despite her nervousness. Good old Tommy.

As soon as the lobby had totally cleared out, she quickly unzipped the gym bag. Halfway open, the zipper caught on a loose thread. Jen panicked, yanking on the zipper with all her might. Pretty soon someone would figure out that Tommy was only joking about the rat, and they'd all head back this way.

Finally the zipper pulled free. She quickly pushed aside the white towel and grabbed the handle of the large gold cup, lifting it onto the middle shelf of the cabinet. Carefully, she pushed the glass door closed. With Zeke's towel draped over her arm, she slung the now-empty bag over her shoulder and breathed a heavy sigh of relief. The relief lasted only a second because she suddenly noticed fingerprints on the shiny gold surface. Some of those were from her hands! If the police checked them . . .

Glancing around to make sure the lobby was still empty, she pushed open the case and rubbed the cup with Zeke's towel until all the prints disappeared. She closed the glass doors once again. Now she could relax.

A strong hand suddenly clamped down on her shoulder.

Jen jumped.

"What are you doing?" a woman's harsh voice demanded.

6

The Phantom Captain

Heart pounding, Jen whirled around. A stocky woman with pale brown hair pulled into a ponytail and black plastic-framed sunglasses pushed on top of her head glared at her. Yellow sunblock covered her nose, but the rest of her face looked deeply tanned and wrinkled.

"What do you think you're doing?" the woman demanded.

"I—I," Jen stammered. "I was just dusting the trophy."

The woman looked doubtfully at the towel. "Wasn't that trophy missing a little while ago?"

"Yeah," Jen said, looking around for Tommy. A few people were drifting out of the cafeteria, chatting about the horrible rat joke. "But someone found it. Isn't that great?" She tried to smile.

The woman's frown cleared. "Yes, that's wonderful," she said, sounding relieved. "I'm so glad it was returned safe and sound."

Jen looked at the woman curiously. She wasn't from Mystic, Jen was sure. But why would an outsider care so much about their trophy?

"I hope Captain Till puts a lock on this case now," the woman continued in her raspy voice.

"You know Captain Till?" Jen asked, heading for the doors that led out of the clubhouse. She didn't want to be there when everyone saw the gold cup in its original place. There would be too many questions.

The woman smiled and held out her right hand as they walked. "I'm Sally Shaw, captain of *The Phantom.*"

Jen stopped and gasped. "*The Phantom?*" Realizing that she seemed rude, she hurried to shake Captain Shaw's hard, calloused hand. Then she continued on and pushed through the doors. As soon as they got outside, the woman flipped her sunglasses down over her eyes.

"You've heard of my boat?" She sounded pleased.

"Oh, yes," Jen gushed. "You arrived today, right?"

"Uh, that's right," Captain Shaw replied.

"I noticed your boat anchored out in the harbor. Why don't you anchor it at the docks with the others? There's plenty of room," Jen added, motioning to the still-empty docking space.

The woman shrugged. "We like our privacy, that's all." Her eyes seemed to be scanning the swarms of busy boaters trotting up and down the path to the clubhouse, over to the docks, and out to the parking lot. Jen couldn't be sure, though, because of the dark glasses that covered the woman's eyes.

Thinking fast, Jen said, "Your boat is beautiful. Could I come aboard and see her up close?"

Captain Shaw shook her head. "I'm afraid not. Only crew is allowed on board. You understand, right?"

"I guess so," Jen said, trying not to sound disappointed.

With a slight smile, Captain Shaw saluted her and hurried away. Jen watched the woman until she disappeared into the crowd. What was so special about *The Phantom* that she couldn't have a tiny peek at it? Was the captain trying to hide something?

Mulling this over, she absentmindedly headed closer to the waterfront. Even though she didn't like sailing, she did admire the graceful lines of a sailboat.

A loud voice caught her attention, drawing her thoughts away from the rise and fall of a sailboat out at sea. Over to the left, at the end of dock one, she caught a glimpse of Salem Dickey, a crew member on the *Regal Wind*. She recognized the obnoxious young man from last year's race in Newport. His mistakes— *practical jokes*, as he called them—nearly set one boat on fire and practically drowned one of his fellow crew members last year. Jen had seen Salem around for the past couple of days, but she'd been trying to avoid him.

The crowd near the *Regal Wind* shifted and Jen groaned. There was Stacey with her notepad, scribbling down everything Salem said. Jen ran over to her friend, but before she could say anything, Salem raised his voice even louder.

"That's right, this old lady is going to win the race this year," he said, patting the dark blue hull of the *Regal Wind*. "With my help, of course," he added, with a ridiculous wink at Stacey.

Jen bit her tongue. She grabbed her best friend's arm and dragged her up the dock. "Don't waste your time listening to him," she said.

"Why not?" Stacey asked, tucking her reporter's notebook into the back pocket of her shorts. "I'm doing a story for the school paper."

"Because all he does is brag," Jen said. "Besides, I have even bigger news." When her friend's eyes lit up, Jen quickly added, "But you can't put this in the paper." Then she described how Zeke had found the gold cup in his *locked* locker and how she had returned it to the case with Tommy's help.

"Wow," Stacey said. "Are you sure I can't put that story in the paper?"

Jen lifted one eyebrow at her friend.

Stacey held up her hands in defeat. "Okay, okay! Where's Tommy now?"

Guilt pierced Jen as she looked around. He was nowhere in sight. "I don't know, but he must be okay, don't you think?"

"Unless Captain Till put him in the brig," Stacey said, using the nautical term for jail, "for starting a rat scare."

"Jeez, I hope not."

Stacey laughed. "I'm only kidding."

Jen smiled, but she couldn't help worrying about Tommy. He'd done her and Zeke a favor. Hopefully he hadn't gotten in trouble for it.

"At least no one saw you putting the trophy back," Stacey commented as they strolled along the path that bordered the marina.

Jen stopped and put a hand on her friend's chubby arm. "But someone *did* catch me! That's what's weird. The captain of *The Phantom* snuck up behind me right after I put the cup back, but she didn't do anything about it."

"What's *The Phantom*?"

Jen positioned her friend to have a clear view out into the harbor. "There," she said, pointing to the distant ship with the leaping dolphins emerging from the prow. "See it?" She waited till Stacey nodded, then added, "It looks just like the boat Zeke thought he saw in Poseidon's Triangle last night!"

"Cool figurehead," Stacey said, shading her eyes from the sun to see it better.

"It's even prettier up close, I bet. In fact, I really wanted a tour of the boat, but the captain said no, absolutely not, no way. I don't know why Captain Shaw is so secretive about the boat."

Stacey grinned at her friend. She lowered her voice to a loud whisper. "Maybe because the ship really *is* a phantom."

Jen couldn't help the shiver that ran down her back at those words. They were ridiculous, but then why had she been thinking the exact same thing?

The Mysterious Six

"I want to get another look at *The Phantom*," Jen said as they walked along. "We can take out a Zodiac. You know how to steer one, don't you?"

"Sure," Stacey said. "But what are we looking for?"

Jen bit her lip. "I don't exactly know," she admitted. "But I've got a weird feeling about it."

"Whatever you say." Stacey turned toward the rental shack where club members were allowed to sign out Sunfish sailboats, kayaks, Zodiacs, and other water gear.

"After we check out *The Phantom*, we'll head for the coves," Jen planned out loud.

Stacey interrupted with a wave of her hand. She pointed to a large sailboat tied up to the third pier. "That is the most beautiful boat here."

Jen had to agree. The *Rakassa* was a seventy-five-foot double-masted sailboat. She didn't know a lot about sailboats, but she did know this one was extra special. Not only was it sleek and elegant, but Zeke couldn't stop talking about it when it had first sailed into Mystic Bay several weeks ago.

"She's a pretty one, isn't she?" a voice asked right beside them.

Jen turned to see who had spoken. Right away she recognized Joe, the captain of the *Rakassa*. She'd seen him around before, and Zeke had pointed him out to her. Besides, with his bald head and bright flowered Hawaiian shirt, he was hard to miss.

"It's the most beautiful boat here," Jen agreed.

"Come aboard for a tour?" the captain asked.

"Definitely," Stacey said, leaping onto the deck through the gate in the railing, with Jen following closely behind.

The captain nimbly jumped aboard. "This beauty is made of teak wood. She's sturdy and heavy enough to withstand the fiercest storms. They don't build them like this anymore," he said proudly.

"Are you entered in the race?" Jen asked.

The captain laughed. "No, sirree. This old gal is far too big and too heavy to compete with those little pip-squeaks."

"She does look a lot bigger," Jen said, eyeing some

of the other sailboats tied up along the docks.

"And too heavy. I could throw all the furniture and half the decking overboard and the *Rakassa* would still weigh too much for this race. The lighter the boat, the faster she'll go."

"She's still beautiful, even if she is fat and overweight," Stacey said with a grin.

"Want to go up for a look around?" the captain asked, pointing to the top of the taller of the two masts.

Stacey shook her head. "Uh, no thanks. I really don't like heights."

The captain shrugged. "Then come belowdecks and see the cabins." He led them down a short set of stairs and showed them the lounge area and the tiny galley where the food was prepared. Then he led them down another staircase. "This is one cabin. Four can sleep in here. The other side is just like this one."

Jen peeked into the cramped room. The two sets of double bunks looked rather narrow, and there were railings on the sides. A small porthole was open, letting in a refreshing, salty breeze.

Next he showed them the tiny bathroom, mentioning that they had to conserve freshwater even though there was a machine in the engine room that converted salt water into fresh.

"And this is the master suite," the captain said, flinging open the double doors at the end of the narrow passage.

Jen and Stacey gasped in amazement. It looked almost as roomy as Jen's lighthouse tower bedroom! A large bed stood against one wall, several portholes let in natural light, a sofa and two armchairs sat around a coffee table, and a doorway led to the bathroom that actually held a whirlpool tub!

"Brother," Stacey exclaimed. "I wouldn't mind sailing on this ship if I could stay in *here*!"

The captain laughed. "I'm afraid this is the owner's cabin. And luckily, I'm the owner!"

Still laughing, he led them topside. He patted the railing. "This old gal has carried me south to Cape Horn, east to the Greek Islands, west as far as Hawaii, and north to Mystic, Maine!"

"And of course Mystic is the best place you've ever been, right?" Stacey asked with a wide grin.

"You said it."

Jen ran her hand down the rail. It was smooth and warm. She knocked on it, hearing the dull thud of solid wood.

"Thanks for the tour," Stacey said, hopping back onto the dock.

"It's a beautiful boat," Jen added, following her

friend with a hand up from the captain.

"Many thanks. Come back anytime," Joe said.

Jen and Stacey waved, then headed for the rental shack where they signed out a Zodiac and life jackets. Luckily, Stacey knew how to start the motor. Jen sat in the front of the rubber boat and held on to the line, just as she had with Zeke.

Stacey expertly steered toward *The Phantom*. "It's almost as pretty as the *Rakassa*," she shouted above the roar of the engine.

"Not nearly as big, though," Jen answered. Movement on the deck caught her eye. Squinting against the wind blowing in her face, she slid her gaze slowly from one end of the boat to the other. She couldn't believe it.

Waving her hand, she motioned for Stacey to slow down. When the engine quieted, she said, "See the people on board?"

Stacey stared, and a moment later replied, "I see them, but so what?"

Jen pursed her lips. "There are six people, and not one of them is Captain Shaw."

"I don't get it," Stacey said with a shrug.

"There can only be *five* people on the racing crew, including the captain. Who are the extra people?"

"Could they be friends?"

Jen shook her head. "I don't think so. Captain Shaw said only the crew was allowed on board."

Stacey revved the engine. "Let's go to the coves before they think we're snooping. They might think we're spies for the Mystic team and try to get the *North Star* disqualified."

Jen nodded in agreement, but as the Zodiac veered south, she caught a glimpse of a familiar hunched figure standing next to the mast. She craned her neck to get a better look, but the hunched man slipped out of view. Could that have been the same man she and Zeke had seen snooping around the docks last night? What was he doing on *The Phantom*? Surely he couldn't be a crew member, could he?

"Ahoy, maties," a voice called as the Zodiac raced toward the coves.

Jen looked to her left, shocked to see Captain Sally Shaw zooming along next to them in a smaller Zodiac. The woman motioned for them to slow down. Jen and Stacey glanced at each other and shrugged. It couldn't hurt to hear what the captain wanted. Maybe she was going to invite them aboard *The Phantom* after all.

"Just heard there's a storm whipping up north of here," Captain Shaw called over. "It'll be pretty dangerous to be out now. You'd better head back in."

Jen shivered. The last place she wanted to be was in a tiny blow-up boat in the middle of a storm. No way, no how. And even though the sky looked perfectly clear, she knew how quickly bad weather could blow in off the Atlantic.

"Let's go back," Jen said to Stacey.

Stacey turned the motor so that the Zodiac swung completely around. Captain Shaw did the same. Before they headed back to the marina, Stacey called over to the captain, "*The Phantom* is a beautiful boat. I love the figurehead."

Captain Shaw nodded and smiled.

"Think we could get a tour of it?" Stacey continued.

Captain Shaw's smile seemed to tighten.

"I'm a reporter for my school newspaper. I'm doing a story on this race, featuring some of the boats."

"I'm afraid that's impossible," the captain said, readjusting the sunglasses on her nose. "I only allow crew on board. You understand, don't you? There's an awful lot of money riding on this race."

"That's for sure," Stacey agreed.

Jen knew her friend was pressing the captain not only for the newspaper, but because Stacey knew Jen wanted a close-up look. She silently thanked Stacey, even though it hadn't done any good. For some reason, Captain Shaw wanted to keep everyone away from *The Phantom*. Except for the mysterious six people she'd just seen on board, that is.

"We saw your crew on board a little while ago," Jen called over. "I forget, how many are there on a team?"

"Five per boat," Captain Shaw answered. "That's me and four others."

Jen bit her lip to keep from saying anything about the *six* people she had just seen on board. Luckily, Stacey stayed quiet, too. Instead of speaking, she opened up the engine and the Zodiac surged forward. Jen almost flew backward, saving herself at the last minute by grabbing the rope.

The ride was bumpy, as though the storm was already blowing in, even though the sky still looked clear. Relief washed over Jen as they finally neared the docks. Just as quickly, that feeling vanished. On the dock where the *North Star* was tied up she saw Zeke surrounded by Tommy and the kids competing for the crew position. Right away, she knew her brother was in trouble.

The Joker Revealed?

Zeke clenched his fists. "I didn't do it," he insisted.

Liz looked at him with narrowed eyes, a smirk pulling at her lips, her arms crossed over her chest. "You were in charge of stowing the life vests last night. Now they're gone. Who else could have done it?"

"I don't know," Zeke said. He barely noticed when Jen and Stacey hurried to his side. Then he turned to the only other boy on the crew. "Unless you know something about this, Chris?"

The smaller boy's eyes widened. "Me? No way. I—"

"Chris," Zeke interrupted, "I know you've been up to something."

"You can't prove anything," Chris said hotly.

Zeke shook his head. He hated to do this, but if he didn't confront the real culprit, he would be blamed for all the "practical jokes" and probably get kicked off the crew.

"How do you know Chris is the one?" Tommy asked, taking a step closer.

Zeke turned to his best friend. "At first I couldn't figure out who would steal the gold cup and put it in my locker to make me look guilty."

Liz and Clara gasped in unison.

"You had the cup all along?" Clara asked, her usually soft voice full of anger.

"No!" Zeke exclaimed, running a hand through his thick hair in frustration. "Well, I guess I did. But I didn't know I did. Someone else put it in my locker." Again he turned to look at Chris. "You did."

Chris opened his mouth, but nothing came out.

"You're the only one who could have put the trophy in my locker in the *men's* locker room. With this race coming up, it's way too busy around here for a girl to sneak in without being caught. And you've been hanging around me so much, I figured out that you must have seen my locker combination over my shoulder."

"No way," Chris protested. He took a step backward. "It's not true. I—I . . ." His voice trailed off as Zeke kept staring at him. Chris looked down at the wooden planks beneath his blue boat shoes. "You're right," he admitted, barely above a whisper. "I did it."

"And the fake call to Tommy, and stealing the notes out of my backpack, and soaking the ropes in seawater and then tying them in knots, and now hiding the—"

"No!" Chris exclaimed. "It's true I called Tommy's house, and I took your notes so you couldn't study and I'd do better on the test than Liz and Clara, and I stole the trophy just in case I didn't ace the test, but I didn't tie the ropes or hide the life vests. You have to believe me."

Liz snorted. "You've got to be kidding, you little twerp! Everyone was giving me the evil eye, and you were the one all along!"

Clara stood to the side, her eyes wide behind her glasses.

Zeke didn't say anything. Even though Chris sounded sincere, how could he trust him after he'd just admitted to so much of what had been going wrong lately?

At that moment, a woman with dark sunglasses perched on her green nose stepped forward. "Is there a problem here?" she asked sharply, crinkling her leathery forehead.

"Hi, Captain Shaw," Jen said. Giving Zeke a look, she said, "She's the captain of *The Phantom*."

Zeke studied the woman more closely. She sure looked normal. Nothing sinister or ghostly. "Hi," he said. "We're just trying to figure out what happened to some missing life vests."

Captain Shaw frowned. "Someone stole them?"

"They're over here," Liz called from the deck of the *North Star*. "They were stowed in the wrong locker."

Zeke shot a look at Chris, but the boy looked as surprised as everyone else.

"Thank goodness," Captain Shaw said. She dug some sunblock out of the pocket of her windbreaker and dabbed more of the thick, green goo on her nose. "We don't want any trouble, do we?"

"I think everything will be okay from now on," Zeke said.

"That's great." Without another word, Captain Shaw hurried toward her Zodiac.

"I wonder why she cares?" Jen mused out loud.

"She was just trying to be helpful," Zeke said. "After all, even though we're competitors, we're still all sailors."

Jen laughed. "You sound like you're giving a speech at an award ceremony."

"And he will be," Captain Saber announced as he approached, a batch of papers fluttering in his hand. "Zeke, you made the crew. You received the highest score on the written exam, and your sailing skills are outstanding."

"All right, Zeke!" Tommy cheered, clapping him on the shoulder.

"We have to tell him about what Chris did," Zeke said. "You should get another chance to try out, Tommy."

Tommy shook his head. "Don't worry about it. I never would have aced the written test like you did."

"What about Chris?" Captain Saber asked, looking from one person to the other for an answer.

Chris finally spoke up himself. "I'll tell you all about it, sir."

Zeke and the others left Chris and the captain alone.

"I knew you'd make the team!" Jen said, walking beside him. "Do you think Chris did move the vests and snarl the ropes into knots?"

"He didn't admit to it, but who else has a motive?" Zeke asked. The twins had solved enough mysteries to know that whenever someone was doing something wrong, that person always had a reason, or motive, for doing it.

Jen shook her head. "Why would he tell the truth about some of the things, but keep lying about others?"

As she kept talking, Zeke listened with half an ear

while going over in his mind all the things he had to do to prepare for the big race. He'd have to get new shoes, a blue *North Star* shirt, and a pair of white shorts. Captain Saber had said he wanted the whole crew to look sharp. He'd have to hurry if he wanted to get some of this done before practice in forty-five minutes.

"Jen, I have to get going," he interrupted.

"Don't you even care about the mystery?" Jen asked.

"What are you talking about? I solved the mystery and Chris admitted to it."

"But what about all the things he didn't admit to? And what about *The Phantom*? Why won't Captain Shaw let me or anyone except her crew on board? And who's that hunched-over guy? And—"

Zeke cut her off again. "I don't know, and I can't think about that right now. I'll see you later." With that, he jogged off toward the bike rack.

An hour later, Zeke curled his toes in his new deck shoes. Already he felt like an official member of the crew. They were out of Mystic Bay now, heading south, as they would for the big race. He loved the gentle bobbing motion of the waves as seagulls soared above them in the clear blue sky, almost as though they were racing against the *North Star*.

The adult crew members congratulated him on winning the competition.

"It's great to have you on the team," Jane said, patting him on the back. "According to your aunt Bee, you're the best sailor around—and very responsible."

Zeke blushed. Aunt Bee was always saying stuff like that about him and Jen.

Now, with the wind filling the sails and the sun nearing the end of its path across the sky, he felt great. He'd made the crew and he'd uncovered the plot against him. Even so, a little niggling doubt wouldn't leave him alone. What if Jen was right? What if Chris wasn't responsible for those other pranks? And what about *The Phantom*? He'd been so sure he'd seen a boat just like it disappear in Poseidon's Triangle. Was it just a pod of dolphins, or was it a boat? And was there really something sinister about a captain who didn't like visitors?

He shook his head and grinned to himself. Now he was getting carried away, just like Jen!

As Captain Saber shouted an order, Zeke snapped to attention, concentrating on his job, his worries forgotten. He grabbed the sheet, ready to pull, when it was suddenly yanked through his fingers.

9

Sea Monster!

"Careful!" Captain Saber shouted. "Zeke, what's going on? Pull it in, pull it in!"

For a few moments, there was chaos. One of the other crew members hurried over to give Zeke a hand. Not until everything was secured did Zeke have a chance to wonder what had gone wrong. One second he was doing what he was supposed to do, the next, the rope was running through his left hand like liquid fire. Who hadn't prepared the sheet properly? Was this one of Chris's leftover jokes?

Now that the excitement had died down, he had a chance to examine his hand. The rope had burned his palm, leaving it red and sore. The friction had even melted the skin a bit, so that it was hard for him to straighten his fingers all the way.

"You okay?" Captain Saber called over to him.

Zeke nodded, slipping his injured hand into his pocket. He didn't want to get kicked off the crew just because of a lousy rope burn.

"We can't have any mistakes like that during the race," the captain warned with a grim look on his face.

Zeke gulped. "No, sir," he replied. He knew it wouldn't do any good to blame it on someone else. Somehow, he'd have to get to the bottom of this before the race. A foul-up like that on Saturday would probably make them lose. And it would all be blamed on him!

The sky looked like milky black ink by the time Jen left soccer practice. She'd been so intent on the upcoming race, she'd almost forgotten about practice. Now she was sweaty and tired and ready for some of Aunt Bee's famous cooking.

She flung her backpack over her shoulders and climbed onto her bike. As she pedaled off, waving to the other girls on her team, her thoughts returned to the phantom ship Zeke had seen. If only she could find some clue as to what it could have been.

Even though she was tired, she headed for the docks. One last look around wouldn't kill her.

The moon was just breaking out from behind

some trees when Jen reached the marina. Coasting slowly, she rode along the path and away from the clubhouse. She was just about to head for the B&B when a strange glimmer caught her eye. Stopping her bike away from any overhead lights, she blinked out toward the sea. For a stunned moment, she couldn't breathe. Way, way out, on the other side of Mystic Bay, she could just make out the shape of a skeleton of a boat. It seemed to float above the dark water, and it was headed full speed, right for the cliffs! In the next second, it disappeared!

Scrambling to turn her bike around, she headed back toward the marina. She dumped her bike outside the front door and ran into the small safety patrol room.

"A ship," she gasped. "I think a ship just crashed into the southern cliffs."

Mr. Rollon leaned back against the desk and crossed his arms. "Jen, how are you?"

"No, really, I saw it. Come on, we have to go help!"

Mr. Rollon nodded, but he didn't move. "I haven't heard any distress calls. I'm sure it was just your imagination. A little bit of moonlight on the water probably."

"Maybe they didn't have time to get out an SOS," Jen argued.

With a sigh, Mr. Rollon moved away from the desk and turned a dial on his marine radio. He called out to all open frequencies, asking if anyone was in danger or had spotted any kind of accident along the southern cliffs. Only a succession of negatives cackled back over the speakers.

"See?" Mr. Rollon said, resuming his former position. "You simply saw a trick of the moonlight."

Jen frowned. It must have only been the moonlight, but it sure looked like a sailboat. The phantom ship.

"There," Aunt Bee said, taping the end of the gauze bandage. "The aloe and tea-tree oil will work wonders on that burn," she assured Zeke.

Jen shivered. Her brother's hand looked sore and red. So far they hadn't had a chance to talk about the accident, but she knew Zeke well enough to know that something like that wouldn't have been his fault. Sure, accidents happened, but Zeke was too careful a sailor to be so clumsy. Something else was definitely going on, just like she'd suspected! And she couldn't wait to tell him about the phantom boat she had seen.

"Come on, let's go play Scrabble in the parlor," Jen said. "Unless you need some help?" she asked Aunt Bee.

Aunt Bee waved her hands, shooing them off. "No, no. When I'm this busy, sometimes it's easier just to do everything myself. You did bring fresh towels to the Rose Room, though?"

Jen nodded. She and Zeke helped Aunt Bee at the B&B by carrying luggage, cleaning the rooms (which were all named after flowers), sometimes helping at mealtimes, and doing any other odd jobs that needed finishing.

"Then go, but don't stay up too late. Remember, you have school tomorrow, and tomorrow night we'll have our hands full!"

Jen grinned. Friday night Aunt Bee was hosting a prerace dinner party. The dining room would be packed, not only because the race was such a big deal, but because everyone in Mystic knew Aunt Bee was the best cook around. It would be so crowded, in fact, that she had hired some women from town to work in the kitchen and help her serve. And Detective Wilson, the retired police officer who was always willing to lend Aunt Bee a helping hand, was now busy stringing festive lights along the gutters outside, even though it was after eight o'clock.

With a swirl of her flowered skirt, Aunt Bee turned and headed back toward the kitchen, her long gray braid swinging back and forth. Jen and Zeke headed for the parlor. Slinky followed them and settled between Woofer's giant sheepdog paws. The cat purred and nuzzled Woofer's nose till the dog woke up and licked her.

Jen set up the Scrabble board, but her mind wasn't on the game. As quickly as possible, she told Zeke all about the Zodiac ride she had taken with Stacey that afternoon.

"Are you sure you saw six people on board?" Zeke asked doubtfully as he formed the word HARDLY across a double-word square.

"I'm positive. I'm also sure I saw the same hunched-over man that we saw sneaking around near the *North Star* last night. In fact," she added thoughtfully, "I saw him on Monday walking down Coast Road, too!"

"But *The Phantom* didn't sail in until today," Zeke said. "So how could he be part of Captain Shaw's crew?"

Jen tapped her forefinger on the table. "That's exactly what I want to know!" Then she leaned forward. "And that's not even the weirdest thing."

Zeke could tell his sister had even bigger news to spring on him. "What is?"

Jen told him about the eerie skeleton-looking ship she'd seen that same night before coming home.

"But when Mr. Rollon called to any ships out there, no one was in trouble!"

"So how do you explain it?"

"That's just it," Jen said urgently. "I can't. But somehow, we have to get to the bottom of this."

Friday after school, Zeke rode as fast as possible down to the marina. Captain Saber expected him to help with the boat's final preparations.

Zeke's first job was to touch up the paint on the main mast. Using the winch, the captain hoisted Zeke up to the top of the mast with a small bucket of paint and a brush.

"Just yell when you need to be lowered," Captain Saber shouted up to him.

Zeke looked down. A single rope was all that held him, way up in the sky. Every tiny motion of the boat below him became magnified. If he let go of the mast, he was sure the swaying would fling him out into thin air.

He swallowed hard. This wasn't exactly his idea of fun, but if it meant being a part of the crew, he'd do it. After several deep breaths, his heart slowed and the sweat on the back of his neck cooled.

Still clutching the mast with his injured hand, he

tried to relax and look around. The water seemed far, far below him. From up here, he had a great view of the marina and harbor, and he could even see well into the old section of Mystic. People bustled around below him on other boats, along the docks, hurrying in and out of the marina, but the most interesting view was looking out over the harbor toward the Atlantic. In the distance, white sails looked like dots of icing on a blue cake. Closer in, he admired the sleek lines of *The Phantom*, still anchored in Mystic Bay.

"She'll be a hard one to beat," he said to himself. So far none of the other boats worried him too much. But *The Phantom* was new to the race and looked very fast, though he couldn't figure out why the crew hadn't taken her out for a trial run. In fact, he hadn't noticed them practicing at all. From up here, the deck even looked deserted.

He shrugged. What Captain Shaw made her crew do or not do was none of his business. The sooner he touched up the paint on the mast, the sooner he could get his two feet on deck again. A gust blew, and the top of the mast swung from side to side. Quickly, he began to paint.

When he was finally finished and Captain Saber had lowered him bit by bit down the mast, Zeke breathed a sigh of relief.

"You did a great job, kid," the captain said, squinting up the tall pole. "Couldn't get me up there for all the money in the world, that's for sure."

Zeke grinned. Somehow, that comment made him feel great. "What's next, Skipper?" he asked,

using the friendly name the other members of the crew used for the captain.

"Do you like to swim?" Captain Saber asked, a sly smile pulling his lips.

"Yes," Zeke said, not sure that was the best answer to give. First, painting the mast. And now what?

"Great. Here are a mask, snorkel, and fins," the captain said, handing Zeke a mesh bag full of equipment. "I want you to scrape the hull. It shouldn't be too bad, but the cleaner it is, the faster and smoother the sail." He slid his hand through the air as though to demonstrate.

Stifling a groan, Zeke changed into his swimsuit, wishing he had his wet suit handy, and donned the fins. He slipped off the far side of the deck, nearly losing his breath in the cold water.

"Don't get between the boat and the dock," Captain Saber warned, leaning over to look down at him.

Zeke nodded, trying to keep his teeth from chattering. He put on the mask and adjusted the snorkel. With the flat scraper in his right hand, he took a deep breath and dunked under. Using the flippers, he propelled himself deeper so he could get at the bottom of the hull. It looked completely clean to him, but he wasn't about to tell Captain Saber that.

Captain Saber would have him cleaning out the bilge next!

Slowly Zeke exhaled. His lungs full of air acted like a life jacket, pulling him up. Careful not to get crushed between the boat and the dock, Zeke quickly worked his way around the hull, scraping anything that looked even remotely green. He rose to the surface whenever he needed fresh air.

Suddenly something moving a few feet away caught his eye, and he thought his heart would stop. Sharks didn't hang out around here, did they?

Zeke had to get some air. He shot to the surface, gasping for breath, realizing he had panicked for no reason. There were no such things as sea monsters, right?

Taking another deep breath, he dove down, scanning the murky depths of the harbor for whatever it was that he had seen. There! A dark shadow caught his attention. Zeke stared. It wasn't a sea monster, or even a shark. It was a man dressed in a wet suit with air tanks, mask, and flippers. The diver held something in his left hand. The object glinted whenever a shaft of sunlight pierced the watery depths.

Suspicious, Zeke followed him, staying behind and higher than the man. This way, he could catch breaths of air as he swam. When the diver extended one hand to check his air tank gauge, Zeke got a clear view of the object: a hand drill! The metal bit sparkled. In a flash, Zeke realized that the man was going to drill a hole in the hull. In the *North Star*'s hull!

Angry, he kicked his flippers back and forth, trying to lunge forward. He reached out, but at the last moment, the diver twisted in the water. Now face-to-face, all Zeke could see of the man were his eyes, strangely distorted behind the mask. Zeke grabbed at the drill and missed. He was about to try again when the diver suddenly caught Zeke's arm and yanked him deeper into the water!

10

The Bribe

Zeke struggled to get away. He tried to tug his arm free, but the diver had a deathlike grip on his wrist. Zeke twisted. If he didn't surface right away, he'd run out of oxygen!

In a frantic last attempt, Zeke dropped the scraper and swung his free hand around. He grabbed the man's mask and yanked on it. Bubbles erupted, clouding the water. He was sure he'd pulled off the attacker's mask, but he still couldn't get a good look at his face.

With his lungs burning and white spots dancing in front of his eyes, Zeke tugged free of his captor. He shot up and exploded through the surface, flinging back his mask and gasping for breath.

"Done scraping?" a voice above him asked.

Trying to catch his breath and tread water at the same time, Zeke looked up at Captain Saber. "Yes, but I dropped the scraper and couldn't get it back."

The captain frowned.

"I'll buy a new one to replace it," Zeke added quickly.

"Okay," Captain Saber said. He looked like he was about to add something, but frowned and shook his head instead.

His heart sinking, Zeke didn't know what to say. It didn't matter anyway because the captain retreated from the edge of the boat. Zeke slapped the water. This wasn't fair! First, Chris caused problems for him, and now this crazy scuba diver. If he didn't watch out, he'd get kicked off the crew. Maybe if he could find the mysterious scuba diver, he could explain to Captain Saber what had really happened. He didn't want to go to the captain with another phantom encounter that he couldn't prove.

With a hopeless sigh, Zeke clambered onto the boat, looking around to see if the mysterious diver had surfaced. There was no sign of the attacker. Zeke hadn't even gotten a clear look at the diver's face. How would he ever recognize him?

After he'd dried off and asked Captain Saber if there was anything else he could do, he hopped off the *North Star* and hurried to the bike rack. He jumped on his bike and headed back to the B&B.

With everything going on tonight, he knew Aunt Bee would need his help.

Sure enough, as soon as he entered through the kitchen Jen said, "It's about time you got home. Help me fold these napkins."

Zeke put down his backpack and sat at the kitchen table, which was covered by a bumblebee-patterned tablecloth. As he folded the blue cloth napkins, he told Jen about his underwater adventure.

She stared at him with wide eyes when he described the attack and how he didn't get to see his attacker's face. "Do you think *he* recognized y*ou*?" she asked.

Zeke's heart sank. He hadn't even thought about that possibility. He'd been so focused on finding the diver, he hadn't realized that if the diver recognized him and found him first, Zeke might be in big trouble! The man wouldn't want anyone around who had seen him under the boats with a drill in his hands!

"I don't think so," Zeke said, thinking carefully. "I had a mask on and a snorkel in my mouth."

Jen frowned. "It definitely wasn't Chris this time. Someone else is trying to sabotage the race. I'll bet it has something to do with that hunched-over man and *The Phantom*."

"I don't see how," Zeke said. "The guy underwater was definitely younger, and his back was straight as a stick."

"We'll see," Jen said with a shrug. "I saw *The Phantom* out practicing this afternoon. It looks good."

Zeke stopped mid-fold on the second to last napkin. "You did? I saw *The Phantom* anchored in the bay."

Jen lifted one eyebrow. "If we both saw it at the same time, maybe it really *is* a phantom ship."

Aunt Bee whisked into the kitchen at that moment, and Zeke didn't get a chance to answer Jen's crazy comment. In fact, they didn't have another chance to talk privately until dinner. Aunt Bee had a million little jobs for them, the hired helpers had invaded and taken over the kitchen, and before the twins knew it, the banquet guests had started to arrive.

Zeke got to sit at the head table with the rest of the crew of the *North Star*, Captain Saber, Captain Till, and several members of the board of directors for Mystic Marina. Most of his table was still up at the buffet line filling their plates. Zeke had already served himself a salad and some soup, saving room for the roast beef he knew was coming next. He tugged at his tight collar. He didn't mind sitting at the head table as much as he minded the stiff clothes Aunt Bee had ironed and insisted he wear. He pulled again, sticking his forefinger between the collar and his neck. With a sudden popping sound, the top button of his shirt snapped off, bounced on the table, and fell to the floor.

His face burning hot with embarrassment, Zeke ducked down to search for the button.

He brushed his fingers over the wooden floor, searching for the small white circle. He'd just located it under his right pinky when he heard Captain Till sit down in the chair next to his and say, "Come on Billy, just lighten the load a little. It'll make the *North Star* speed like a shooting star. And when you win, there might be a little extra winnings for you."

Captain Saber said, "You know I can't do that. We've all been inspected for tomorrow's race. Making the boat lighter just so she'll go faster is cheating!"

Zeke lifted his head, almost bumping it on the bottom of the table. Captain Till stared at him in surprise, then grinned sheepishly. "So you heard me, eh? Well, can't blame me for wanting to win the race again this year, can you? Of course, Captain Saber is too honest to do anything like that."

Zeke glanced at the captain of the *North Star*, who was glaring down into his clam chowder. Captain Till shrugged, turned to the person on his right, and started chatting about the fine weather they'd been having. Zeke couldn't believe the head of the marina could be so calm about trying to bribe

Captain Saber to cheat in order to win the race. To what else would Captain Till resort to become the winner?

A chill rippled down Zeke's back. Would he send someone underwater to drill a hole in a rival boat's hull? Maybe the diver wasn't after the *North Star* after all.

Taking a spoonful of thick chowder, Zeke eyed Captain Till. The old man looked so much like Santa Claus it was nearly impossible to think of him doing anything dishonest, even though Zeke had just heard it with his own ears.

"What are you shaking your head about?" Jen asked over his shoulder. "Did you find clamshells in the chowder?"

He gave her a look and said, "I'll tell you later." He could tell she understood not to question him about it right now.

She nodded. "Have you found who you were looking for?"

Zeke scanned the room. It was hopeless. How would he ever recognize the scuba diver? Then a face caught his attention. Salem, the obnoxious crew member from the *Regal Wind*, was sitting at a table by the window. When he turned his head, Zeke saw a white bandage taped to Salem's cheek. He pointed this out to Jen.

"Maybe you scratched him when you pulled off his mask," Jen whispered.

Zeke nodded. That's exactly what he'd been thinking, too. "But I'll never be able to prove it." He remembered how angry Salem had been last year when the Mystic boat had won the race, ruining Newport's long winning streak. Salem had sworn revenge, even though no one really took the braggart seriously.

"I just hope he doesn't try something else," Zeke added. "He might get away with it this time."

"But if he is the one you saw underwater," Jen said, "and maybe the one doing the other pranks that Chris didn't admit to, what does it all have to do with *The Phantom?*"

Zeke shrugged. "I don't know, but we both saw some kind of phantom ship out on the ocean, and there have been strange things going on with the real ship *The Phantom.*"

"Do you think they're connected somehow?" Jen asked.

Zeke didn't have a chance to answer because at that moment Captain Till stood up to make an announcement, and Jen hurried back to her seat.

A Midnight Disaster

Jen stared out her bedroom window. Living in the lighthouse tower gave her a perfect view of Mystic Bay. Even though it was the middle of the night, the nearly full moon gave off enough light to give the bay a shimmering glow, and she could see vague outlines of the sailboats at the dock. But it wasn't bright enough to see anything clearly, which is what she really wanted to be able to do. She needed to know what was going on around Mystic before the race started in the morning.

There's only one thing to do, she thought.

Without giving herself a chance to chicken out, Jen quickly changed out of her pajamas and into a pair of black jeans and a dark blue sweatshirt. She pulled on a New York Mets baseball cap, positioning the brim low on her forehead. If she were seen, she didn't want anyone to recognize her.

Tiptoeing quietly, she made her way down the circular stairs to the lighthouse museum on the first floor, crept through the entrance hall, and then slipped out the kitchen door.

She jumped on her bike and flicked on the headlight, then coasted down the steep driveway. The air was cool, and Jen shivered—but she didn't know if it was from the cold or from fear.

"No going back now," she told herself. She had to check out the *North Star* and make sure nothing fishy was going on. Zeke's life might depend on it!

Jen pedaled as quickly as possible to the old logging road into town and down to the marina. As she neared the docks, she turned off her headlight and walked her bike through the shadows to the cluster of ancient pine trees near the parking lot. Stepping quietly over the bed of fallen needles, she left her bike leaning against one of the sappy trunks, well out of sight unless someone went under the branches looking for it.

Several lamps gave off some light along the docks, but most of the boats were dark. Everyone was resting up for tomorrow's big race. Jen crept forward. Everything was still except for the gentle bobbing of the boats. Loose ropes, which she knew she was supposed to call halyards from hearing Zeke talk about it enough, clacked in the slight breeze.

Away from the docks, the water looked dark. Any boats anchored in the bay had only a mast light to warn other ships where they were. No cabin lights gave any signs of life.

Feeling a bit ridiculous for worrying so much, Jen stepped closer to the marina, where she could get a good look at the moored *North Star*. Everything looked okay.

Suddenly the wind carried a murmur of voices toward her, but Jen couldn't pinpoint the exact location of the sound. *Never mind*, she thought. Someone was bound to be awake, even this late. All she had to worry about was the *North Star*. There it was, looking pretty and peaceful as always, right where it was supposed to be.

But wait! Jen gasped as she realized the *North Star* wasn't exactly where it was supposed to be after all. It was drifting away! It was untied, and it was on a path to crash into the dock, or worse, another boat!

Before Jen could start running to the *North Star*, another figure darted out of the shadows. The hunched man scurried down the dock. Could he have untied the *North Star*? If so, Jen was sure he was planning something even worse, now that the boat was loose.

She had to stop him! She sprinted forward just as some voices rose in alarm. Making an instant decision, Jen crouched behind the rental shack, trying to remain hidden. Captain Till and Captain Shaw raced toward the boat. Salem appeared from the opposite direction, the white patch of his bandage bright on his cheek. Along with the hunched man, the four of them used grappling hooks left alongside the docks to catch the sailboat before it did any damage to other boats or got destroyed. Grunting and giving directions to one another in low voices, they managed to drag the boat close enough so that Salem could jump on board.

"Lines have been cut," Salem called softly.

Jen's heart plummeted. *So this wasn't an accident!*

He quickly attached some new line, fastening the boat firmly in place so it couldn't drift away again. When he finished, he clambered off the *North Star*. "I wonder who did that," he said.

Jen gritted her teeth. *Probably you,* she accused silently. Suddenly she realized the hunched man had disappeared. She scanned the area, but saw no sign of anyone.

"I think we should keep this to ourselves," Captain Shaw said, lowering her voice.

Jen turned her head so she could hear better. The brim of her cap hit the side of the rental shack and flew off her head. It plopped down just beyond reach, right in a circle of light from one of the lamps. She didn't dare reach for it. Luckily, no one seemed to notice.

"It might put a damper on the festivities," Captain Shaw continued. "Besides, all the boats have been inspected for the race already. If this gets out, the officials will want to do another inspection, and that'll postpone the start."

Captain Till nodded. "It won't make the Mystic Marina look very safe if this near-disaster gets out. It could mean lost business."

After checking to make sure the ropes were fastened securely, the two headed back to the clubhouse. Jen inched sideways, keeping to the shadows so she wouldn't be spotted.

As soon as they were out of sight, she relaxed. But only for a second. The creak of a board right behind her nearly made her jump out of her skin. Silently, she whipped around. Salem stood not two yards away, staring toward the marina clubhouse and the parking lot, a frown etching lines in his face.

She froze. Because of her dark clothes, he obviously hadn't noticed her there, crouching almost at his feet. She sunk further into the shadows of the building. Jen watched as Salem headed into the shadows, as though he were trying to stay hidden, too. He crept along, clearly searching for something or someone.

When Salem spotted Jen's baseball cap on the ground, her heart started to hammer. He picked it up, examining the Mets emblem on the front. Jen expected him to look straight at her and accuse her of sabotaging the *North Star*. But he still hadn't seen her.

Jen didn't budge as Salem moved on, her baseball cap stuffed into his back pocket. He got closer and closer to the parking lot and to the trees that hid her bike from view. She followed very quietly, keeping a safe distance behind him. She breathed a sigh of relief when he didn't notice her bike. Instead, he circled the entire clubhouse. She half expected him to retrieve the knife he'd used to cut the ropes to the *North Star*, but he never stopped. What was he doing? Who was he looking for? Was he suspicious of the hunched man, too?

After a complete turn around the building, he was right near the parking lot again. He peered under the pine trees. Jen held her breath. Would he find her bike this time? And if he did, would he keep searching till he found her, too?

12

On Board at Last

With Jen's cap still stuck in his pocket, Salem Dickey took one more look around the area, then headed back to the *Regal Wind*, where he jumped on board and went below.

At last. Jen blew out a breath of relief. Salem had found her hat, but luckily he hadn't spotted her. If she hurried, she could be home and in bed in thirty minutes. That sounded awfully tempting, but then another idea came to her.

Beside the last dock, Jen noticed Captain Sally Shaw's Zodiac. Obviously she was still onshore talking to Captain Till. And the hunched man must be somewhere onshore, too, or she'd have heard a motor revving to get away. She peered out into the harbor. *The Phantom* still looked dark. Was anyone on board?

Heart thudding, she crept down to where the clubhouse rowboats were tied up. She couldn't drive a Zodiac, but she did know how to row. Putting on a life jacket, she climbed into one of the aluminum boats, untied the line, and pushed away from the dock. With the oars fitted into place, she headed the prow out to sea and started rowing.

About halfway to *The Phantom*, Jen thought her shoulders were on fire. When did rowing get to be so hard? This no longer felt like an adventure; it felt like work. Sweat dribbled down her forehead. She peeked behind her. It looked like miles to the sailboat, but if she gave up now, she'd never get another chance like this to get on board.

Hunching her shoulders, she kept pulling on the oars.

At last she reached *The Phantom*, and rowed around to the far side—the side out of sight of the marina. The only way onto the boat was the flimsy rope ladder hanging from the deck, nearly touching the water. Standing precariously in the rowboat, with the line in her right hand so it wouldn't drift away, she reached up and grabbed the rope ladder. Luckily, all those hours playing soccer had made her strong; otherwise, she was sure she'd be swimming right now.

Not letting go of the rowboat rope, she climbed

the ladder and flopped forward onto the deck. If anyone was on board, they definitely would have heard the commotion. But only Jen's steady breathing and the soft lapping of waves against the hull broke the silence.

Carefully, she tied the rowboat's line to one of the railing posts. Swimming back to shore did not sound like fun. At last she could look around *The Phantom*. The light on the top of the mast and the moon gave her enough visibility to make her way around the deck.

Compared to the *North Star*, this boat looked rather messy. Ropes weren't neatly coiled, life jackets weren't stowed out of the way, and several empty root-beer cans rolled back and forth with every sway of the boat. Jen frowned. She had thought Captain Shaw would keep a neater boat.

Jen worked her way to the prow. Besides the sloppy conditions, which she knew Captain Saber would never allow, she didn't spot anything suspicious. This certainly didn't feel like a phantom ship. The decking was solid, as was the mast, which she knocked on as she passed. She reached out to pet the leaping dolphins that made the figurehead. The wood felt smooth under her fingers. Smooth and solid, like the teak railing on the elegant ship *Rakassa*.

She had been so sure there was something fishy

about this boat. Disappointed, she was about to try the cabin door when she heard a faint throbbing sound. An engine! And it was getting closer!

Panicked, Jen knew exactly what it was: Captain Shaw returning in her Zodiac!

Jen clambered down the rope ladder, landing in the rowboat with a nerve-racking slosh of water over the sides. With fumbling fingers, she picked loose the knot she'd so carefully tied. Finally, she sat down and engaged the oars. Pulling as quickly and as quietly as possible, she rowed away from *The Phantom*, glad she was on the far side of the sailboat and well out of sight.

As the sound of the motor faded, Jen felt sure she'd be safe, and headed in toward the docks. When the metal boat bumped up against the pier, she realized that she could still hear a motor far off in the distance. Surely the Zodiac had reached *The Phantom* by now? Or maybe it wasn't Captain Shaw after all? Jen squinted in the darkness. No, the captain's Zodiac wasn't tied up in its usual place along the dock. So it definitely *was* Captain Shaw in that motorboat, but why hadn't she returned to *The Phantom*?

Too tired to figure out the puzzle, Jen secured the rowboat and hurried back to her bike. Nervous about being caught, she didn't relax until she was home in bed, safe and sound. Then she was too exhausted to do anything more than close her eyes and fall asleep.

When the alarm shrilled in her ear the next morning, it felt as though she'd only been asleep for five minutes instead of three and a half hours. Tempted to turn over and go back to sleep, Jen dragged herself out of bed. She couldn't miss the start of the race. This was Zeke's big day.

By the time she got down to the marina, there were crowds of people jamming the walkways and the docks as the boats prepared to head out to their starting places.

The bike rack was full, so she parked her bike near a bench, along with several other bikes. She'd just put down her kickstand when she felt a prickling sensation along her neck. Uneasily, she looked around. She almost jumped back in fright when she saw Salem Dickey glaring right at her. His eyes moved to her bike. She followed his gaze. The New York Mets pendant hanging from her handlebars fluttered in the breeze.

When she looked up again, Salem had disappeared. Jen swallowed the knot of fear in her throat. Had he figured out she'd been here last night? That he'd found her baseball cap? Did he think she'd seen him cutting loose the *North Star*? Would he try to hurt her to keep her from talking?

13

A Real Phantom?

Zeke scanned the docks for Jen and Aunt Bee. He spotted his aunt with Detective Wilson, and they waved. Grinning, he waved back as the *North Star* motored out toward the starting point. At the last second, he saw Jen. She gave him two thumbs-up. He knew she was wishing him luck.

He turned away from land and looked out to the mouth of the bay where the race would begin. Flexing his fingers, he was amazed that his rope-burned hand felt fine. He silently thanked Aunt Bee and her homemade cures.

A second later, Captain Saber barked out orders. The race was about to start.

Excitement tingled in Zeke's veins. He couldn't believe he was actually part of the crew! But if anything bad happened, he felt sure he'd be blamed. "Nothing can go wrong," he said softly. "Nothing!"

As soon as the race started, Zeke didn't relax for one second. Orders flew at him. He fastened this, then loosened that, then pulled here and pushed there. He barely had a chance to notice that they were in the lead, with the *Regal Wind* not far behind. Not far at all! Way back in the distance, however, he saw *The Phantom*. Obviously the crew of that ship was having problems of some sort. They had slipped into last place.

Finally he started to relax. Even with the *Regal Wind* just to their stern, the tension began to ease away from his shoulders. At least they didn't have to worry about *The Phantom*. He knew that all the boat crews had been worried about that sleek vessel. But with it trailing so far behind, no one had to worry about it anymore. Now he just had to concentrate on following orders and staying ahead of their only real rival: the *Regal Wind*.

Feeling safer now that she knew Salem was out at sea on his racing boat, Jen watched until the last sailboat disappeared from sight beyond the southern tip of the bay. *The Phantom* had started off badly and was well behind by the time the rest of the boats had disappeared from view.

"Now we just have to wait around till they come back," Stacey said. "They're going to have games behind the clubhouse. Coming?"

Jen shook her head and absentmindedly waved to Stacey as she headed off. "Not now. I promised Aunt Bee I'd help out at the B&B." How could she explain even to her best friend that she was worried about Zeke on the *North Star*? Stacey would call her a worrywart, but Jen knew something wasn't right.

All morning, Jen helped Aunt Bee clean up the B&B and prepare a lunch buffet for the guests. The entire time she worked, Jen kept running over the clues in her head. Something strange was going on, she was sure of that, but what? In the afternoon, when Aunt Bee excused her to go down to the marina to wait for the end of the race, Jen eagerly jumped on her bike. But she didn't go straight to the marina.

She pedaled across town to the hiking path that ran along the southern cliffs. They had never really inspected that suspicious bonfire site in ·Hidden Cove. *Could that be an important clue?* she wondered.

Just in case, she had to check it out.

She had to hop off her bike and push it up the steep, rough path many times. Falling over the cliff simply wasn't on her schedule for today.

At each cove, a treacherous trail led down to a rocky beach, or directly into the water. Despite the strong currents, it was easier to enter the coves by boat than to clamber down the trail. And coming back up was even worse.

By the time she reached the lookout point for Hidden Cove, the sky had turned pink from the sunset. Shadows broke off from the cliffs and the dense forest, giving the air a chill. Jen expected to look down into a dark, empty cove. Now that she'd made it all the way up here, she realized she was wasting her time. What clues could she possibly gather from an old campfire way below her?

Balancing her bike beside her, she stared down into the cove. It took a couple of seconds to realize that she wasn't looking down at a rocky beach and a small, empty inlet. The rocky beach still sat there like a dark crescent moon, but the inlet wasn't empty! *The Phantom* sat anchored in the middle of it!

Jen couldn't believe her eyes. What was the racing ship doing down there? Had it had so many problems that it had to pull in for repairs? Or did the current pull it off course? Or— She shook her head. None of that made any sense.

Her first instinct told her to climb down the trail and get a close-up look at the boat. From here, she couldn't tell if anyone was on deck or not. She

thought she spotted the shadow of a hunched-over figure, but she couldn't be sure.

As soon as she examined the trail that led down to the beach, she scratched that idea. Even if she did make it down there without falling head over heels, she'd never make it back up. The only thing to do was to go get Stacey and Tommy. Maybe they could take out a Zodiac to investigate the cove and find out why *The Phantom* was anchored here instead of out racing like it was supposed to be.

Riding as quickly as possible without falling over the cliff, Jen bumped and jiggled down the uneven path. When she hit smooth dirt and finally pavement, she sighed with relief.

As soon as she reached the marina, Jen parked her bike and continued on foot. Crowds of people called to one another and jostled by, talking about the race and making bets about which boat would come in first. Jen raced through them, searching for Stacey and Tommy. At last she found them—next to the hot-dog stand, of course.

Stacey saw her first. "What's wrong?" she asked.

Jen caught her breath. "*The Phantom*! It's in Hidden Cove!"

Stacey started to say something, then she looked over Jen's shoulder and said, "It couldn't be. Here comes *The Phantom* now!"

Jen whirled around. Stacey was right. Sailing into the bay with full sails catching the fading light, *The Phantom* slid toward them like a puff of cloud. Not far behind came the *North Star*.

Her heart fell. Zeke's boat didn't win. She joined the mad rush out onto the docks. *The Phantom* slowed, turned, and anchored offshore as it had before. The *North Star*, however, dropped its sails and chugged to the dock under engine power.

As soon as it was tied up, Captain Till congratulated the crew, but everyone could see that he was sad.

"You tried your best," Captain Till continued. "That's what matters most."

"It would have been nice to win," Zeke added under his breath so only Jen could hear him.

Jen squeezed his arm. Everyone in Mystic had gotten his or her hopes up so high that coming in second was a great disappointment.

"I can't believe *The Phantom* caught up and passed you," Tommy said. "What happened?"

Zeke explained how *The Phantom* had trouble early in the race and dropped out of sight. But about halfway through the race it was spotted way in the distance. It just kept catching up and passing all the other boats until it was tied for first place with the *North Star*. It pulled into the lead at the end of the race.

"*The Regal Wind* isn't in yet," Stacey commented, keeping track in her notebook of all the boats as they arrived.

Jen looked out at the bay. If the *Regal Wind* had been in real trouble, the Coast Guard would have been notified. "Maybe they got lost? The Atlantic is pretty big."

"I'm going to find out," Stacey said, and she trotted off to find the information.

"She's such a reporter," Tommy said. "But I think I'll go with her." He chased after her.

Jen laughed. She knew the only reason Tommy was following her best friend was because he wanted to be there if there was news of some big disaster. Tommy always wanted to be in on anything exciting, unless, of course, it meant missing out on a meal.

Zeke and Jen wandered through the crowd and found an empty bench to sit on. In hushed tones, Jen told Zeke about last night and about what she'd seen in Hidden Cove not long ago.

"So what does it mean?" Jen asked when she'd finished. "The boat I saw looked just like *The Phantom*. So either it really *was* a phantom boat, or—"

"Or you just imagined it," Zeke interrupted, leaning back.

Jen glared at her twin brother until Zeke held up his hands in defeat. "Okay," he said with a grin. "You didn't imagine it. And we didn't imagine the ghostly boats we saw in Poseidon's Triangle, or ramming into the cliffs. So there's obviously something strange going on."

"*Obviously,*" Jen repeated. "But what? And who is involved?"

"How can a sailboat be in two places at once? *The Phantom* was definitely behind us for the last three hours," Zeke added. "And who was trying to sabotage the *North Star?*"

Jen jumped to her feet. "Come on."

"Where are we going?" Zeke asked, following.

Jen headed for the clubhouse. "We need paper to write up suspect sheets. At least that way maybe we can figure out one part of this mystery. . . ."

Mystic Lighthouse

Suspect Sheet

Name: Captain Till

Motive: Seemed so sure of winning. Was he planning something?

Clues: Heard him trying to bribe North Star captain.

Would he do anything to have Mystic win?

Why did he warn us away from the southern coves?

Mystic Lighthouse

Suspect Sheet

Name: Salem Dickey

Motive: Swore revenge on Mystic since losing the race last year.

Clues: He's known for his "practical jokes"

Did he tie the ropes?

Did he hide the vests?

Did he cause Zeke's rope burns?

Was he the one underwater with the scuba gear and the drill? He did have a bandage on his face afterward.

Did he untie the North Star last night?

Mystic Lighthouse

Suspect Sheet

Name: The Hunched Man

Motive: ??

Clues: Why was he sneaking around the boats all the time?

WHAT WAS HE UP TO? DID HE HAVE ANYTHING TO DO WITH:

KNOTTING THE ROPES?

HIDING THE VESTS?

CAUSING ZEKE'S ROPE BURNS?

Did he untie the North Star?

Is he a member of The Phantom crew? If so, why was he here so many days before the boat arrived?

Why did he run toward the North Star and then disappear after they secured it again?

Mystic Lighthouse

Suspect Sheet

Name: Captain Sally Shaw

Motive: To win the race and money

Clues: Did Zeke really see The Phantom in Poseidon's Triangle? If so, what was it doing there?

Captain Sally Shaw was very nice and helpful about any possible trouble going on at the marina, but was gruff whenever Jen asked to tour The Phantom.

Nothing seemed suspicious on her ship, even though it was rather messy, but why wouldn't she let anyone but crew members on it? And why did Jen see six crew members on board?

What did Jen see in Hidden Cove right before the end of the race? Was it just a boat that looked like The Phantom?

When they'd reviewed the last suspect sheet, Zeke frowned. "It's not any clearer to me now than it was before," he admitted.

Jen flipped through the papers. "The answer's got to be here somewhere. We just have to figure it out."

Note to Reader

Have you figured out who is trying to sabotage the race? And how does *The Phantom* fit into all of this? Jen and Zeke have made pretty good notes on the suspects, but they did miss a few important clues. Without those clues, it's almost impossible to figure out what is going on.

Have you come to a conclusion? Take your time. Carefully review your suspect sheets. Fill in any details Jen and Zeke missed. When you think you have a solution, read the last chapter to find out if Jen and Zeke can put all the pieces together to solve *The Mystery of the Phantom Ship*.

Good luck!

Solution

Another
Mystery Solved

Jen and Zeke tried to figure out the clues all the way back to the B&B. They had to change clothes and get ready for the big celebration at the Mystic Marina that night. By the time they got back to the clubhouse, a band played on the lawn, little kids ran around in fancy clothes, parents danced along the docks, and tables of food and drinks were lined up inside and out like cars on a train. People stood around in groups talking about the fireworks display that would light up the sky at nine o'clock.

"This is great," Jen said, enjoying the festive air.

Zeke tried to smile. He knew he should be happier, but he'd been so confident that the *North Star* would win when *The Phantom* had had trouble at the beginning of the race. The entire crew had been shocked when *The Phantom* had slowly caught up and passed them. He still couldn't believe it.

Jen sensed her brother's distress. She turned away from the dancing and said, "If we can figure out the mystery of the phantom ship, maybe you'll feel better."

"Maybe," Zeke agreed glumly.

Jen tapped her foot in time to the music. "How can there be one boat in two places at the same time?" she wondered out loud.

"There can't be. It's impossible," Zeke said.

"Exactly. That means there are two boats that look almost identical."

"From what you say, the boats *were* identical," Zeke pointed out.

Jen stuck a cracker in crab dip. "That doesn't make sense. Why have two of the exact same boat?" She popped the cracker into her mouth and licked her lips. It tasted like Aunt Bee's recipe. As she chewed, she remembered something the owner of the *Rakassa* had said. Something about weight . . . heavier boats . . . solid wood . . . slower . . .

"I've got it!" she exclaimed.

Zeke nearly dropped the meatball he'd just stabbed with a toothpick. He managed to get the sweet and spicy morsel into his mouth without dripping any of the sauce on his shirt.

"I've figured it out! All the sailboats were inspected

and weighed the day before the race, right?"

Zeke nodded, a glimmer of understanding coming to him.

"What if there is a regulation-weight *Phantom* ship and a lighter, faster, *identical* copy?"

"That would be cheating. They'd never win."

"Only if they were caught," Jen pointed out.

"That's why they slowed down at the beginning of the race, pretending they were having problems," Zeke said slowly, putting it all together. "After the crew switched onto the faster boat, they caught up and passed us all."

"Yes! Now we just have to tell Captain Till."

Zeke put out a hand to hold Jen back. "Not yet. If we're wrong, all of Mystic will look like sore losers. First we have to check out our story and make sure we're right."

"All we have to do is go to Hidden Cove tonight. I'll show you the second *Phantom*. I'll bet you anything it's the heavier boat that they hid in the cove during the race."

"I'll go sign out a Zodiac and meet you on the dock," Zeke instructed, taking off in the direction of the rental shack.

Jen waited for Zeke, making sure no one noticed what she was doing. If any of *The Phantom*'s crew saw them, they might get suspicious. At last Zeke appeared with the key for the engine. They hopped in and motored away as quickly and quietly as possible. Zeke didn't open up the engine till they were well away from the docks.

The water was choppy, and Jen felt a northern chill in the air, as though a storm were headed their way. This reminded her of yesterday when she and Stacey had been heading out to investigate Hidden Cove and Captain Shaw had stopped them. Jen suddenly realized that the squall the captain had warned them about had never appeared. Did Captain Shaw make that story up just to keep the girls away from the coves and the hidden ship?

She couldn't prove it, but she felt certain that was true.

Tonight, however, Jen was afraid there was the threat of a real squall. She clung tightly to the rope, glad she had fastened her life jacket extra tight. Once they left the protection of the bay, the wind picked up, and the choppy water suddenly turned into large waves. Nervous, Jen glanced back at Zeke, but all she saw of his face was the dull gleam of his teeth. Her crazy brother was smiling!

Swallowing a groan, Jen crossed her fingers that the Zodiac wouldn't flip over. She even crossed her toes as they passed Poseidon's Triangle. This whole mystery had started there; she hoped it didn't end there, too!

When Zeke finally steered into the mouth of Hidden Cove, Jen breathed a sigh of relief. The sheltered water didn't jump and slap at the rubber boat, but lay calm and friendly.

Zeke turned on the bright spotlight he'd signed out from the rental shack. He swung the beam around the cove while Jen's heart fell. It was empty!

"Are you sure you saw a boat here?" Zeke asked, shining the light across the water again. "Never mind," he added hastily, sensing his sister's anger. "It's gone now."

"We'll have to check out *The Phantom* that's anchored in the bay," Zeke said.

Jen bit her lip. She'd much rather head right back to shore and put her feet on solid ground, but the thought of someone cheating to win the race made her furious. If Mystic's *North Star* came in second fairly, that was one thing. But if they lost because of liars and cheaters . . . "Let's get going."

"Are you sure?" Zeke blasted the light over Jen's face. "You look a little pale."

"Get that out of my eyes and let's move," she ordered, raising her hands.

"Sorry," Zeke said, revving up the motor again.

The ocean felt even rougher than before once they left the protected water of the cove. Glad she'd only eaten a cracker before they left, Jen gritted her teeth, determined not to become seasick.

From a distance, *The Phantom* looked deserted. Obviously, the crew was celebrating at the party. *All six of them and their captain?* Jen wondered. She sure hoped so.

Zeke pulled up next to the ship. The rope ladder hung off the side as Jen had seen it earlier. Feeling sure this must be the same boat she had inspected before, Jen clambered up the ladder, practically falling on her face on the deck. Wearing a skirt made things a lot more difficult.

Zeke boarded after her. "See anything suspicious?" he whispered, even though they were far from shore. Sounds of the party drifted across the harbor.

"It all looks the same," Jen said, peering about. "But someone's cleaned up. It was a lot messier before."

The twins started at the stern and slowly worked their way fore, toward the bow of the sailing vessel. Jen looked at everything closely, but nothing seemed out of place or considerably different from her last visit. Jen reached out and patted the dolphin figurehead.

Zeke and Jen were concentrating so hard on trying to find a clue, they didn't hear the slap of oars in the water come closer and closer. All of a sudden, a voice barked, "What are you two doing?"

Zeke jerked around.

"Grab them," the voice ordered.

Jen shrieked.

Hands clamped onto Zeke's shoulders and he was shoved forward. He tripped, and when he caught his balance, he was staring right into the face of Captain Shaw. Only this time, she didn't look very friendly.

She scowled at him. "What are you up to, kids?"

"I just wanted to see your beautiful boat," Jen said. Zeke heard the tremor in her voice.

"That's right," he agreed. "I love the dolphins on your figurehead. We just wanted to get a closer look."

Captain Shaw narrowed her eyes.

Jen looked at Zeke and shuddered. The hunched man held him firmly by the shoulders. Captain Shaw clenched the front of her own life vest, which she hadn't removed.

"Do you think I'm stupid?" Captain Shaw demanded. "I knew something was going on, so we rowed out here to surprise you. Now I'm going to—"

"Hold it right there!" a deep voice commanded.

A sudden shove sent Jen flying. With a splash and a shock of cold, she landed in the water. Strong hands pulled her safely back on board, and someone wrapped a large blanket around her shoulders to stop her teeth from chattering. That's when she recognized Captain Till and Captain Saber.

"What's going on here?" Captain Till asked when

Jen's teeth stopped chattering.

"That's what I wanted to know," Captain Shaw retorted. "We found these busybody kids snooping around. They're trespassing. I'll report you all to the authorities."

Captain Till shook his head. "I don't think so. Not yet, anyway. Jen, Zeke, why don't you tell me what you two are doing out here?"

Zeke glanced at Captain Saber, who stood as still and silent as a ship's figurehead. "I—we thought there was something suspicious about *The Phantom*," he admitted, realizing how ridiculous he must sound. "We didn't understand how this boat could have been in last place and then finished first."

"Because we're experienced," Captain Shaw said sharply. "We deserved to win."

Jen spoke up. "We're really sorry." She moved forward as she continued. "I just wanted a tour. I guess our imaginations got the better of us." She stroked the dolphin's back a second time. Then she tipped her head. On a hunch, she made a fist and knocked against the carved mammal's side. A pinging sound echoed under her knuckles. The dolphins were hollow!

Captain Shaw coughed, then laughed nervously. "Fine, I won't press charges. But I must insist you all leave at once."

"Wait a minute," Jen exclaimed, knocking on the dolphins again. "These were solid wood last time I was on board."

Captain Till stroked his beard. "You've been on board before tonight?"

Jen lifted one shoulder and nodded. "Last night I snuck on. But last night the dolphins weren't hollow. This must be a different boat. A *lighter* one," she added, remembering what the captain of the *Rakassa* had said about the weight of a boat.

"So it'll sail faster," Zeke added, in case the captains didn't understand what Jen was getting at.

Suddenly all eyes were on Captain Shaw and the hunched man beside her. "I can explain," she said.

No one replied.

"You see," she went on. Then her voice trailed off and she bowed her head.

Captain Till turned to the twins. "I believe when we get the official inspectors on board, we will find that the *North Star* won the race after all!"

Zeke let out a cheer. He couldn't help himself. Jen grinned, too, but she would have been happier if she weren't soaking wet.

As Captain Saber radioed in for help, Captain Shaw admitted to the whole scheme. The reason she didn't want visitors on board was because she was afraid someone might notice something odd about the boat or the crew. For example, the hunched man, whose name was Bob, wasn't a sailor at all.

"That's why I saw six crew members on board the other day," Jen said.

"That's right," Captain Shaw admitted. "We have a racing crew of five, but the others were here to help with the second boat when it wasn't being used."

"And you hid the second boat in Hidden Cove," Jen exclaimed. Now it all made sense. "Zeke saw it disappear in Poseidon's Triangle, but really it was just slipping into Hidden Cove."

"That's right," Zeke said. "And when Jen saw a ship crashing into the cliffs, it was *The Phantom* heading into Hidden Cove after practicing late at night."

Jen grinned. "So we both really did see a *phantom* ship after all."

Zeke turned to Bob. "Did you tie the knots in the *North Star's* ropes and hide the life vests?"

"And cut the lines last night?" Jen added.

The man shook his head. He glanced at Captain Shaw. When she nodded for him to continue, he said, "I didn't do anything like that. I just wanted to see what the competition looked like. I know who did all those things, though."

"Who?" Jen asked, surprised.

Zeke held up his hand. "No, don't tell us yet. I figured out Chris was trying to sabotage the junior crew member competition by prank-calling Tommy and doing some things to me, but he didn't play all the so-called jokes. It must have been Salem Dickey from the *Regal Wind*."

"That's right," Captain Shaw said. "Bob told me what he'd seen, but how did you know?"

Zeke grinned. "When I took out the Zodiac tonight, I asked who had rented scuba equipment lately. The only person who had was Salem."

"For all the trouble he was causing," Captain Till said, "he should have been paying more attention to his own duties."

"What do you mean?" Jen asked.

Captain Till couldn't hide his smile. "He was supposed to tend to the sails, but he didn't. One of them ripped because of his carelessness. The *Regal Wind* never even finished the race! We won't see *him* back in Mystic for a long time!"

Jen and Zeke looked at each other and laughed.

"I have to ask you," Jen said, looking at Captain Till, "why did you warn us away from the southern coves the other day?"

"Because they're dangerous, of course."

"No other reason?" Jen asked.

The captain shook his head, looking confused.

"And what about when I heard you trying to bribe Captain Saber to lighten the *North Star*?" Zeke added.

Now the white-haired gentleman looked sheepish. "I'm not proud of that," he admitted. "But I knew Billy Saber had far too much honor to go along with me. I just meant it as a little joke, though I'm sure to you it sounded dishonest." He leaned toward the twins. "I hope we can simply forget about it? I promise to never joke around like that again."

"Sure," Zeke agreed, and Jen nodded.

Then Zeke said to Captain Saber, who had just returned from the radio room in two long-legged strides, "I hope you didn't think I was responsible for any of those mistakes, sir."

"Don't worry about it, Zeke. Now that I know the truth, I know you're not only the best junior sailor, but you and your sister are the best detectives around, too!"

With that, the sky lit up in a spectacular display of fireworks.

Everyone except Captain Sally Shaw and Bob cheered.

"So how does it feel to be a winner?" Jen asked her brother.

Zeke smiled. "Oh, it's okay, I guess!"

About the Author

Laura E. Williams has written more than twenty-five books for children, her most recent being the books in the Mystic Lighthouse Mysteries series and *Up a Creek*.

Ms. Williams loves lighthouses and, like Jen, gets seasick in sailboats. Someday she hopes to visit a lighthouse bed-and-breakfast just like the one in Mystic, Maine.

Mystic Lighthouse

Suspect Sheet

Name:

Motive:

Clues:

**Join Jen and Zeke
in these other exciting
Mystic Lighthouse Mysteries!**

The Mystery of
Dead Man's Curve

The Mystery of
the Dark Lighthouse

The Mystery of
the Bad Luck Curse

The Mystery of
the Missing Tiger

Coming Soon:

The Mystery of
the Haunted Playhouse